T0065612

The Elementals:

The Beginning & the End

The Elementals:
The Beginning & the End

Sharada M Subrahmanyam

PARTRIDGE
A Penguin Random House Company

ISBN:	Hardcover	978-1-4828-4913-4
	Softcover	978-1-4828-4912-7
	eBook	978-1-4828-4911-0

To order additional copies of this book, contact
Partridge India
000 800 10062 62
orders.india@partridgepublishing.com

www.partridgepublishing.com/india

Chapter 1

Date: the fifth day of the month of Lena, 2013

Report number: 1001

Subject: The Duels

It was the last day of school.

I was sitting next to my mother, Liana Paula, sipping a glass of water and smiling a smile that I was sure didn't reach my eyes. I somehow had this feeling, this premonition that something really, *really* bad was going to happen.

If only I hadn't been right.

Mom, as usual, was very optimistic.

"Bye Ella! Don't worry, nothing can go wrong."

Only mom. She was being, well, optimistically pessimistic. She told me that nothing could go wrong, which meant that she thought that I thought something might go wrong, which meant that she, obviously, was, at some level or the other, worried, either subconsciously, or consciously, and felt that she shouldn't worry me. Which worried me.

Nonetheless, I forced another smile, and laughed her off. "Obviously. See you soon, mum!"

As soon as I reached school, I saw my best friend, Fleur Bluma. She was an energetic, ever smiling person, and was a genius when it came to – well, everything. She had a way with plants, flowers, studies, books – you name it. She was peaceful, and somehow made everyone near her laugh.

"Ella!" She crushed me in a hug. "Last day of school!" she laughed as she pulled away. "How awesome is that? And guess what? Sol's coming after school!"

Sol is Fleur's friend, but she never stops talking about him, which makes me suspect they might just be more.

"That's great," I told her. "But let's get through the day first. I mean, Progress reports!"

Fleur laughed. "Well, it can't be that bad. After all, you did have me helping."

We shared a smile, but then the teacher walked in. I groaned. Progress reports.

Looking back, I miss the time when progress reports were my biggest worries.

"Bluma, Fleur. First rank." Called the teacher, smiling. I clapped, grinning. Fleur had a way with teachers as well.

The teacher went on calling names, until-

"Paula, Eleanor."

I got up, waiting for her to read out my rank. She looks up and smiles at me. "Second rank."

My jaw dropped. Second! I smiled and went to collect my card. "Well done, Eleanor." She murmured quietly. "Ella," I said, equally quiet.

"Ella." She said, smiling.

The rest of the day progressed fairly quickly, and it was soon time to leave. Before I could leave, however, I was stopped by someone slamming into me head on.

I blinked. Then I sighed. "Pam." Pam Nicola was the third rank, and she, obviously, felt that I shouldn't have gotten second rank, or even passed.

"Ella," she said in a high pitched, mocking imitation of my voice.

I raised my eyebrows. "Do you need to see the nurse? You sound like a rubber duck that's been stepped on."

She colored. "I didn't see you this cocky yesterday in math."

Now it was my turn to color. I'd forgotten to bring in my homework, which you, obviously, don't want to do. I smiled sweetly. "I think you mistake calmness for cockiness. Of course, no one blames you, dear."

She snarled. "Don't insult my intelligence."

I tilted my head. "Don't insult mine, and we have ourselves a deal."

I walked past her, and she decided to take it a step further. "Where're you going, crying to your dad? Oh, wait, you're going to your mom! Momma's girl!" She jeered. I clenched my fists and turned around.

"Oh? And what about you, Nicola?" I raised my eyebrows. "Going to run to your daddy? Tell him that you can't handle someone standing up to you, since you're a bully?" Wind whipped my hair around, but I didn't care. Until I noticed that I was in the middle of a mini tornado.

Thankfully no one noticed, and I turned around and walked away, taking deep calming breaths, praying no one noticed. I stepped out, and let out a breath.

"Where were you?" snapped Fleur. "Sol's here."

I pursed my lips. "Two words: Pam Nicola."

She winced in sympathy. "Sorry."

There was a brief silence. I looked at Sol. He had golden yellow eyes that looked like he had two suns staring at you. He had wavy hair that looked gold where the sun struck it. I held out my hand. "Hey, you must be Sol."

"Yeah. Sol Soliel." He exchanged a glance with Fleur.

"Yeah," I laughed, ignoring the look. "Fleur's told me all about you."

Sol raised his eyebrows. "All good, I hope."

I grinned. "Maybe!" We laughed.

Sol turned to Fleur. "Will you go get the others?"

Fleur nodded. "I'll go directly to camp after that. See you both!" She waved and disappeared. Literally.

"Whoa! How did she *do* that?" I demanded, my eyes wide.

"All in good time, kid. Maybe." He grinned.

"Who're you calling a kid? You're my age!"

"Sure." He snapped his fingers. Everything disappeared, and we appeared in a forest.

I shook my head. "How-"

Sol grinned. "Because I'm awesome."

I snorted. "Of course. Not because I'm dreaming."

Before he could retort, however, there was a wave of flowers, and four others appeared.

"Fleur's in. That's good." Sol said cryptically.

"In where?" I snapped, tired of not getting my questions answered.

Sol shot me a look. "In camp, of course."

"Camp?" I questioned.

Sol sighed. "Fleur didn't say anything, did she?" I blinked, and he sighed again. "I guess not."

I turned to the other four and introduced myself. "Hey, I'm Ella!"

A girl with red hair and eyes that looked like fire grinned at me. "I'm Feira."

I grinned back. "Suits you!"

"Gabriel," said the other girl. She had brown eyes and hair. "Nice to meet you."

The third person had blue eyes and black hair. "Mojada."

The last guy had striking grey eyes. "Luftal."

"Hi!" I said, grinning.

"*If* we're done," Sol snapped.

"Sorry, Sol!" The five of us turned to him.

"Now, remember that you must not get distracted. Don't focus on anything around you. Think of nothing. You could get lost if you don't, so please, make sure you listen to me."

We nodded, but I was confused. Why did he need us to do that?

Sol said few words, which I couldn't catch, and a wall of colors appeared. There was every color, every shade imaginable, and the light that was the colors kept shifting.

Just then, the shadows seemed to darken. From them stepped out a pale boy with black hair and black eyes, as deep as the deepest ocean, if not deeper. Sol pushed the five of us back, glaring at the newcomer.

"Cattiva Mauvaise." He spat the words venomously. "What do you want?"

He smiled, though it didn't seem pleasant. "You."

A lot of things happened at once. Both Sol and the boy – Cattiva – snapped their fingers. Feira, Gabriel, Mojada, Luftal and I were thrown back, falling not onto the wall, as expected, but rather right through it.

And Sol?

Sol and the boy disappeared through the shadows, and wherever they went, I suspected it wouldn't be great, at least not for Sol.

Chapter 2

As we shot through the wall, I noticed the vivid colors, the beautiful shades, and thought, *if this is lost, then I wouldn't mind it at all.*

Then I nearly smacked myself. Of course I would feel that way. Isn't that what Sol said? I closed my eyes, and cleared my mind. *Think of nothing.* I thought. *Focus on nothing.*

And as suddenly as we were thrown into the wall, we were thrown out.

"Where's Sol?" I looked up (yes, I fell. No, don't say anything!), and stared into the eyes of a girl with long black hair. It was uncannily like mine, and her eyes were like mine as well – never settling in one color, shifting like it can't decide, first blue, then green, then light brown – well, you get the idea.

I shrugged. "I have no idea. He must have come here – wherever this is. Who are you?"

"Juliet Elementa. You are in camp Elementals. Tell me exactly what happened," she ordered.

I nodded and told her exactly what happened. When I was finished, Juliet nodded and turned around. "Follow me." We did, and we heard her mutter to herself, "...used his power...going to kill Cattiva...what was she thinking..." I don't know what *Juliet* was thinking, and I don't want to know.

I looked around. It almost seemed like another world, and I'm not being pessimistic when I say, the grass is greener on the other side. There was a wide plain, with lots of trees and grass. There were a lot of kids playing around, which would look innocuous, except they were playing with sharp things. Not sharpeners, or pointy pencils, or anything that tame. They had swords, and daggers, and spears. I caught up with Juliet. "Swords? Spears? Knives? What is going on?"

She didn't slow down. "If you get an amulet, all will be explained."

"Amulet?" I demanded, annoyed beyond belief.

"Come." She walked ahead, I glared at her back, annoyed.

I continued looking around, and noticed a place that seemed to have a lot of sparks (if you could call it that) in them. There was an arena, and large houses. And Juliet called this a *camp*?

There was also an Auditorium, I noted, and that was where we were going. The kids I noticed playing with sharp things were following us there, as well as a bunch of others. The Auditorium was filled by the time we got there. Juliet turned to the crowd.

"Friends!" She called, and the crowd quieted down. "Today, five have Come to us. Let us see what Goes to them." *Looks like today is the day for cryptic messages,* I thought, annoyed.

She brought forward a collection of 12 amulets, and placed them in front of us. There were some interesting things there – a tornado, a flower, a small flame, a – was that the earth? – and a drop of water, amongst other things. Four of them moved – the Earth, Air, Fire and Water. Predictably, they went to Gabriel, Luftal, Feira and Mojada respectively. Immediately, the crowd started talking. I heard a few snippets.

"Isn't that the Elements?"

"They're all Elements, Regen."

"No, those are *the* Elements."

"No way!"

"Way. I mean, look at Juliet! She's white!"

I looked at Juliet, and found that whoever said that was right. She gestured towards the ceiling. Two more amulets emerged – one black and one white. The black one had white lines, and the white one had black lines. They both had 12 small pictures, for lack of a better word, around their edges. Juliet took them in her had and placed them in front of me. Slowly, the white one emerged, and a black thread materialized behind it. It tied itself to my right hand, and I looked at Juliet.

She was expressionless.

"Hail, Feira Le Feu, of Fire. Hail, Mojada Auga, of Water. Hail, Gabriel Tierra, of Earth. Hail, Luftal Lucht, of Air. And hail, Ella Elementa, of the Elements. Welcome to Camp Elementals."

I don't know about the others, but it sure didn't feel like a warm welcome.

<hr />

Juliet introduced me to her apprentice, who, oddly enough, was called Apprendista Elementare. I raised my eyebrows, and she grinned. "Apprendista is my title, sort of." I nodded, grinning back. Juliet told her to give me the tour, and ran off to do something or the other.

Apprendista turned to me, and we started chatting like we've known each other forever. Of course, it was more like a question answer session, but it was still more than I've talked to anyone other than Fleur.

Finally, there was a brief lull in my questions, and Apprendista told me other things I should know.

"So, basically, Camp is divided into 13 parts – Earth, Air, Fire, Water, plant, Flower, Sun, Moon, Gems, Animals, Stars, Colors, and Elementa - the White Magic ones."

"White magic?" I interrupted.

"There are, broadly, two categories of Magic – White and Black, but better expressed as Light and Dark. They are separate and, usually, incompatible. But, of course, all Magic has a touch of the Other. Like, in your amulet, you can see the lines between the Elements is black, the color of Dark Magic. That shows that you are also a bit Dark, apart from Light. The amulets are a source of power, kind of like a rechargeable battery." I blinked at that comparison. Not something one would expect to describe Magic. "Here, this pamphlet shows exactly where to charge & how you can tell if it is charged." I put the paper in my jacket pocket and looked up. Now she became serious. "Listen Ella. Whenever there are more than one Elementa at the time, there will be *war*. Careful, Okay? Don't meddle with The Dark Side too much."

Ok, I've got to admit I got a little spooked. A war because I came? That is seriously weird. But, hey, I've seen weirder (Like at the school, for example. I did create the tornado after all.). But moving on with the report (believe it or not, that's what this is!), Juliet decided to take me to the Elementa's house. Apprendista told me to meet her at the home of the Apprentices (Maison de l'apprenti) if I needed anything. Then she vanished into thin air. Literally. It was like she faded out. I grinned. Maybe I could do that too!

Following Juliet's instructions, I went to the Magos Verdaderos (house of the Elementas). Flashy name? I thought so. On entering, I turned back and faced nothing but a big brick wall. Hmm. Odd.

I sat and waited. Juliet hadn't arrived yet, so I decided to explore a bit. I put my hands in my jacket pockets, and brushed my hand against some paper. I pulled the pamphlet out, and pursed my lips. I'd forgotten about this. I sat down on the sofa and read through it.

Welcome to Camp Elementals, <u>Ella Elementa</u>. Seeing as you are now an Elemental, we at Camp Elementals thought that you could use some help in figuring things out. Your amulet probably needs to be charged. Given below is the list of places where you can charge your power or powers, as the case may be.

Power	Place to charge	What the magic looks like
Air	Permanent storm	Small tornado
Water	Little whirlpool	Stream of clear water
Fire	Flame in a glass sphere	Orange jets of fire
Earth	A rotating model of earth	Dark green streams of glitter with streaks of mud brown
Plant	A tree that glows at night	Light green streams of glitter
Flower	8 flowers	Colorful stream of glitter
Sun	Carving of sun on stone wall	Gold stream of glitter
Moon	Carving of moon on stone wall	Silver stream of glitter
Colour	Ring of colors around everything	Rainbow coloured stream of glitter
Precious stones	8 Stones floating in a crystal ball	Blue stream of glitter
Animals	Carving of animals on wall	Red stream of glitter
Stars	Night sky permanently above.	Stream of stars in deep blue background

Please bear in mind that other things can renew the magic. The place described above is for convenience. To make sure that your amulet still has some magic, tap it thrice. It will glow for 10 seconds and then stop. If that does not happen, charge it IMMEDIATELY. When full of the required magic, it will glow for 30 seconds and then stop. If we have a new addition to camp, then the amulet will glow briefly.

Best of luck,

Juliet Elementa,

Julietelementa

Apprendista Elementare,

Appelerenmendistartae

I tapped my amulet thrice, and sighed. It glowed for about a millisecond, before it stopped. I decided to go charge it, and turned to the brick wall. I stared at it. *How, exactly, am I supposed to go charge my amulet, or go out at all?* I thought, annoyed.

Immediately, a door appeared. I raised my eyebrows. Cool.

I went out, and found myself in a room where everything described in the amulet was there. *This must be the place where I saw the 'sparks',* I realized. I saw the magic flow into me, in jets and streams. The magic was mesmerizing, mixing together, separating, forming a pattern, moving to another, flowing as smoothly as water flows down a smooth hill. It was so enchanting that I didn't notice when someone else joined me.

"Pretty, isn't it?" I jumped, startled. It was a boy of about sixteen, with black hair. He was seemingly innocuous, but for his eyes – deep, dark, and drawing me away from my body. I blinked, breaking myself out of the trance.

"Who are you?" I demanded.

He laughed softly. "Malvagita Ubella," he whispered into my ear. I flinched. How did he come there so fast? "Now run along, Eleanor Paula Elementa," he whispered, sending shivers down my spine. "Tell Juliet that I am back." He touched my shoulder, and a black mist spread from his hand onto the rest of my body. I jerked away, and fell down. Malvagita smiled. "Another time, Ella. Soyez En Sommeil." He waved his hand, and I felt my eyes close, and darkness wash over my conscience.

Chapter 3

"Not now, Juliet!" Someone was saying. "I understand if you're worried, but you need to wait for her to wake up, not wake her up!"

"Too late." I muttered. Unfortunately, they heard.

"Ella!" Said Juliet, sidestepping the person in front of her. "What happened? I tried to wake you up, but Luna didn't let me. Who did this? Was it someone from camp? How-"

"First of all," I interrupted, "breath. Secondly, How am I supposed to know if he's from camp? I know he isn't, but even so, it's, no offence, a dumb question. Thirdly, will you wait for me to answer, or just keep asking questions until I forget what you asked?" I paused. "Good. Now, he had black hair, black eyes as deep as the pits of hell, and seemed to be around sixteen. He said his name was Malvagita Ubella." I said this calmly, but internally, I was hyperventilating. Who was this boy? Where did he come from? And why on earth was Juliet so pale?

"Thank you, Ella," said Juliet, her voice seemingly calm. "You have no idea how much this information helps."

The other girl, Luna, reached for Juliet's shoulder. "Juliet…"

"It's starting." Juliet's reply was short.

"What's starting?" I asked getting off the bed.

Juliet looked at me with pity. "The war."

After a lot of pleading and arguing and begging, I finally managed to convince Luna to let me go. I was feeling downright energetic, and any more time in bed would drive me absolutely crazy.

Suddenly, the air seemed to turn colder. *Ella Elementa...*The wind seemed to whisper. *Join us...join me...*

"Ella!" Juliet called, and the moment was gone as soon as it came. "How did you get out of the infirmary?"

"Easy," I replied with a grin. "I'm not infirm."

Juliet snorted, and I cracked another smile. "Well?" She asked, eyebrows raised. "Questions?"

"Just two. My mom…"

"Knows. She was a wind Elemental, and one of the best in history. And the second?"

I hesitated, and straightened. "How can I help?"

Juliet smiled. "Let's go train, shall we?"

We went to the training arena I had seen when I came to camp. We went and sat in a corner of the arena, and Juliet instructed me to close my eyes. "Master your mind before you attempt to master your body," she said. We closed our eyes, and meditated.

I soon got bored, and started fidgeting. I opened my eyes and looked around at what the others were doing. There was a pair of Star Elementals dueling in the corner, and I watched them. They didn't seem to be using their swords much, rather, swaying on their feet, jerking back, and occasionally twitching like something just shot past their head. *Interesting,* I thought. *I wonder why –*

My train of thought was interrupted when I noticed a slight shadow on my left. I looked right at it, and noticed that there was nothing that seemed to be casting the shadow. I narrowed my eyes, and blinked.

What was *Cattiva Mauvaise* doing in camp?

Suddenly, there was a scream, and my head snapped towards the sound. A black mist seemed to be covering one of the Star Elementals, and the other was whispering frantically, seemingly trying to stop it.

I turned to back to Cattiva, who didn't seem to notice me. I walked over to him, and hear him whisper a few words under his breath. *"Take you...Estrella...come..."*

I growled. He had done enough! I did a three sixty, making him fall. He looked up at me, confused. "How can you see me?" He demanded, scowling.

"Oh, I don't know. Maybe because I have eyes?" I said sarcastically.

"Who are you talking to, Ella?" Juliet asked.

"What is it with people and stupid questions? Cattiva Mauvaise is right there!"

Juliet narrowed her eyes, and said, "Faccio il non visto veduto!" Make the invisible visible.

Wait, how did I know that?

Everybody started following her cue, but Cattiva snapped, "Compaia! Coltello!" Which I somehow understood meant, Appear and Knife.

And it was a good thing too, because a second later, Cattiva was standing behind me with a knife under my neck. "Weapons down!" He called, pressing the knife closer to my neck. I decided to try the oldest trick in the book.

I stepped on his foot. The results were unexpected.

He yelped, jumped back, and tried (and failed) to throw his knife at me. "Bloccaggio!" I yelled. Capture. Then I blinked. *How did I know that?* I wondered, not for the first time that day, and certainly not the last.

A golden-orange net wove around Cattiva, effectively trapping. As though that weren't enough, the net lifted him up, so that he dangled up a few feet in the air.

I turned towards where the Star Elementals had been. The mist had faded, and the girl looked relieved, leaning against the wall for support. Her friend stood by her side, giving her water, and generally fussing over her.

I turned to Juliet, who looked even more confused than she had a moment earlier. "How did you know the spell?" She asked.

I shrugged. "No idea. It just popped into my mind." I felt a thousand eyes bore into my back. "And by the way you all are looking at me, I'm going to hazard a guess and say that that is not normal."

"Too right it isn't!" Snapped someone behind me.

"Oh, leave her be, Bogen." Someone else snapped.

"Fleur?" I asked, wide eyed.

"Of course. Who else could it be?"

I grinned. A familiar face, at last! I said as much, and Fleur smiled. "Would you have been just as relieved if the familiar face had been, say, Pam Nicola?"

"Ugh, no!" I snapped, shuddering. "Don't even think about it. She's horrible!"

Fleur laughed. "Well, yes, but you did say-"

"Not another word, Fleur."

She raised her hands. "Alright."

"Have you heard of Der Estre Magier?" Juliet cut into our conversation.

I was about to say, *no, duh,* but my hands moved of their own accord. Golden mist flew out of my hands, forming the words, *Ich bin Der Estre Magier.* I am Der Estre Magier.

There were gasps all around the arena. Juliet grabbed my arm, and we went to the Magos Verdaderos.

"Der Estre Magier, would you do the honors?"

There was a slight breeze, and suddenly, a woman of about twenty-one appeared next to me. She sat down.

"I am Der Estre Magier. Sit down, Ella, Juliet. We have a lot to discuss."

Chapter 4

"Tell me," Estre turned to me, "What has happened?"

"Well," I started, and then I couldn't stop. The words just flowed out of me, until finally-

"And now we're here. What is going on?"

Estre was silent for a long time. "A war." She said finally. "It is a war, but there's something different, something inexplicable going on here."

"The missing people?" I cut in.

"Perhaps. You two need apprentices."

I looked at Estre oddly. "*I* need to be trained first, Estre."

She smiled. "Don't worry. You have my knowledge and experience, though not my memories. Take Fire. She is very powerful."

Suddenly, Apprendista ran into the room. "Jules, Mauvaise is in the Maison de l'apprenti. I don't know what to do!" The poor girl seemed to be in the verge of hysterics.

"Calm down, Elementare," Estre said soothingly. "Any guesses as to how he came there?" Apprendista shook her head.

"I think," I said slowly, "I know." The others turned to me. "He used a spell to leave once I released him, right?" I got some affirmative nods. "Versile?" More nods. "It means home. Maison de l'apprenti is the home of the apprentices, and he is an apprentice. Hence," I flashed a grin, "the result."

Estre nodded. "That makes sense. We'd best go banish him." With that, she disappeared.

Estre? I thought.

Yes.

What's a banish? Why was Cattiva here in the first place? How do I have your knowledge, but not your memories? Not that I'm complaining. But-

Ella. She cut my tirade off. *I'll answer your questions later, alright?*

But the Banish-

Sortez. Banish in the Language of Magic. Since Cattiva is a dark apprentice in his home, we need three people doing the Banish. As for why he is here...I fear we will not like the answer.

I entered the Maison de l'apprenti. *Capture.* Estre instructed me.

"Bloccaggio."

And Cattiva was in the net again.

"Why are you here?" I demanded, glaring at Cattiva.

"And what," he said silkily, "makes you think I would answer you?"

"Me." Estre stepped forward.

Cattiva's eyes narrowed. "Der Estre Magier. A pleasure. Not."

"By the Laws upon which the Elementals existed," Estre continued, ignoring Cattiva's interruption. "An apprentice can be captured and questioned if the essence of the Elementals is threatened, and your master, Mauvaise, has done that. So now tell me, why are you here?"

Cattiva glared at her. "Scouting territory."

"You don't need it, Mauvaise." Spat Juliet. "You know this place as well as I do."

He raised his eyebrows and smirked. "Is that so?"

Juliet opened her mouth to answer, but Estre raised her hand. "Enough, Juliet. He is telling the truth." She turned to Cattiva. "Where is Sol Soliel?"

"No idea." Came the prompt reply.

She sighed and waved her hand, making the bonds disappear. Immediately, the rest of us raised our hands. "Sortez."

And he disappeared, leaving behind a message in the black smoke that was in his wake.

Another time, Ella Elementa.

Chapter 5

Juliet was in a somber mood the rest of the evening. Finally, after I had thoroughly explored the place, she called me there. "I have an idea, but I need your help executing it."

"Let's hear it," I told her, sitting on the sofa.

"Can you ask Estre to put up a shield first?"

I nodded. *Estre?*

She came out, and smirked. "I'm not completely unaware of what's going on here. Ni l'un ni l'autre ne nous regarderont." She cast the spell. I made a mental note to ask her about it later.

It means, she told me. I jumped. *Only part of me outside, Ella. The spell ensures that neither Malvagita nor Cattiva can See us with their powers.*

Ah.

"Your plan?" I asked out loud.

Juliet took a deep breath. "I'm going to give the leadership of the Elementals to one of you."

There was a pause. "A good plan," Estre finally qualified. "Ella would be better suited to the task that I would."

Juliet nodded. "No one would expect a new girl to be the leader." She turned to me. "Are you willing?"

21

I hesitated. Was I, more importantly, ready?

You are, said Estre. *The fact that you think about this says more than you could.*

I nodded resolutely. "Yes."

We held hands. "I, Juliet Elementa, do hereby transfer my title of the Leader of the Elementals to you, Ella Elementa."

"I, Ella Elementa, accept the responsibility that you give me, and do hereby swear to uphold the honor and principles upon which the Elementals stand." I didn't know where the words came from, but they did.

"So mote it be." They finished together.

"Ella will officially take over from you if you get captured."

"When, not if," she said grimly. "I expect I'll be taken near the end, the captain of a sinking ship."

Estre nodded. "I fear so. Well, I take leave."

She disappeared. *Now, Ella, its time for you to take an apprentice.*

I nodded to Juliet and left. I went to the Fire place, and knocked on the door. "Hi, Ells!" Feira let me into the room. "What's going on?"

"Nothing much. Just wanted to ask you a question."

She grinned. "Well, ask away!"

"Will you be my apprentice?" I asked bluntly.

She blinked once. Twice. Then she shrugged. "Sure. When'll we make it official?"

Before I could answer, a shadow passed over the room, and gathered at the center in a dark sphere. I raised my hands, and Estre summoned a sword in my hand.

Suddenly, two shots of black mist shot towards where we were standing. I raised the sword, and the mist ricocheted back into the sphere. *How did I do that?* I thought.

No time to think. Two more shots flew at us, and I raised my sword again. This time, I managed to deflect one, but the other one brushed against my arm and hit the wall behind me. Immediately, another shot came and struck me on my shoulder. I lost my grip on the sword and stumbled to my knees. I tried to get to my feet, darkness threatening to swallow me. The shadows surrounded Feira, extinguishing the balls of fire that she had summoned as a defense.

"*Didn't I tell you,*" came a soft voice near my ear. I flinched, throwing a fireball in the general direction of the sound. "*I told you that I'd be back.*"

"Leave her alone, Malvagita. She has nothing to do with this."

"*She is an Elemental, Ella Elementa. This has everything to do with her.*"

I felt a searing pain in my shoulder. Some shadows pulled out of there. The presence in the shadows seemed to chuckle. "*Another time, Ella Elementa.*"

"Think of something else to say, why don't you?" I snapped, annoyed that I couldn't fight him better.

The room cleared, and I stalked towards the door. I went to the Magos Verdaderos, finding Juliet there. "And so they strike again," I said sourly. "They took Feira." I explained what happened.

Juliet was silent for some time. Then she said, "Let's go."

"Where?" I demanded, following her out of the room.

"To train."

First, we went and got a sword and shield for me. Then we proceeded to the training arena, the place where people were playing with these sharp objects.

"Though the Elementals typically rely on their magic for everything, it's always best to be able to defend yourself with something physical. Your magic isn't always reliable, and it's best to have a backup plan. And the most successful and powerful Elementals have always somehow managed to combine both, to weave a spell with their weapon. I've tried to make the Elementals use their weapons, and judging by what you've told me, it's a good thing too. Are you ready?"

"No."

"Let's begin, then." She ignored my negative response.

First, we began with the parts of the sword – the pommel, grip, and crossguard on the hilt, and the fuller, edge, central ridge, and point of the blade, the forte and the foible of the blade, even the parts of the sheath – the locket and the chape. Then, sadly, we moved on to the actual dueling. I thoroughly embarrassed myself.

"Guard! No, not like that! I can get to you like that! Point up! Why are you slouching? Move your feet!" By the end of the thing, I was red from fresh bruises, tiredness, and embarrassment. Juliet summoned water for herself using her amulet, and raised her eyebrows at me. I closed my eyes, and thought, *water?*

A small yell made me open my eyes.

"Maybe," said a dripping wet Juliet, "we need to work on your control, hmm?"

I nodded emphatically. "Yeah."

And thus, I got myself into another vigorous training round. I couldn't keep my mouth shut, could I?

By the end of the day, I was tired, hungry, tired, annoyed, tired, bored, and oh, did I mention tired?

As we were walking back to the Magos Verdaderos, we heard a yell from the corner. I glanced at Juliet, and we ran towards the source. A familiar cold feeling overtook me. "Malvagita," I whispered, horrified. I drew my sword, and whispered a reveal spell. "Apparaissez."

Malvagita shimmered into existence, along with another boy with an amulet that identified him as a rainbow Elemental.

"Bogen!" Shouted Fleur, elbowing her way to the front of the crowd.

Malvagita ignored her. "I shall meet you in battle, Ella Elementa." He stated, a cold smile worming its way onto his face. And with that, he disappeared.

Chapter 6

Normally, I would have been thrilled at the thought of meeting Fleur in any place during the holidays. Then again, I wouldn't have been magical and would not have just seen Bogen and Malvagita disappear. I would also not be the one consoling Fleur, like it was that day.

"Look, Juliet." I said wearily. "All I saw is Bogen and Malvagita. He said we would most probably meet in battle. Then they disappeared, leaving behind a few wisps of smoke."

"You saw absolutely nothing else?"

"Nothing."

"You sure?"

"Yes!"

"I did." I was shocked to hear Fleur speak in that hoarse voice.

"What, Fleur?"

"There was a message. 'The most precious is next' was floating above his head in rainbow colors."

"That would be the person who has the precious stones' amulet."

Fleur and Juliet looked at each other and said simultaneously, "Stein Kostbare."

"We need to give him a little more protection. Also, It could be you, Juliet, as being the lead Elementa, you are quite important in maintaining the balance. So extra protection for you too."

"I am quite capable of taking care of myself, thank you very much."

"So was Bogen."

"How do you know?"

"Well, it is very, very difficult to project a message while captured by dark forces. So, I guess you can call Bogen powerful."

"Fine." She huffed.

You're getting better at this, Ella.

Thanks, Estre.

Now, We forgot one little thing.

What, Exactly?

Well, they know you know what we will do next. So they can very well change the plan.

They won't.

How do you know?

I hid us.

Good!!!

Estre, could you shield me from them for the rest of the day?

Sure.

I spent the rest of the day designing a protection device, which was basically a bead. I filled one with some power and tested it. I made sure the thing would not harm a living thing, only capture. I animated a few dummies by influencing the straw in them using the plant part of my amulet. I had them walk towards me and then threw the bead at them. It exploded into a hurricane, which ripped them apart. Also, a few wisps of white mist surrounded them in little white spheres. That was designed to keep the Dark thing from reforming. Cool, huh?

I made many of these and then did test two. I strung them and pulled one of the beads. None of the other beads came off, but the one I pulled did. I threw it at a spear. The bead grew into a storm, ripping the spear apart. Then the mist did its job. I made another bracelet with an equal number of beads. These were capable of taking in the powers again. I reabsorbed the storm and mist in one of the beads and slapped it into the other bracelet. I also made the beads come back to the original number by putting an Everlasting kind of spell on them. I made another pair like this and asked Estre how it was.

Well, Ella, you also have to make sure it is impossible steal it, to lose it, and stuff like that.

I knew I forgot some thing!!

Then why did you not do it?

'Cause I didn't know what I forgot!!

I did that and then asked for more evaluation.

Good. Give one pair to Juliet and the other to Stein.

Okay. Shield still on?

Yeah.

I went to Juliet and gave her a pair. She said, "Why on earth would I need jewelry!?!"

I told her all about the beads. She was impressed. She then sent me to Stein to give it to him.

I went to the place where he lives and entered with no difficulty. As soon as I entered I knew it was too late. There were wisps of black smoke that showed a message - Kostbare is taken.

Chapter 7

Great. After all the trouble I had gone through to make the protection beads, it turns out that the one I made it for is taken. It's almost like Malvagita knew what I was doing. But he couldn't have, because Estre did a do not see me kind of spell. The spell might have weakened, but that was impossible, as Estre was the equivalent of four magicians. The only other possibility was a spy in the room, which is impossible, as that particular place was extremely private. Neither possibility was good.

I decided to concentrate on making the beads and getting them to the people. I finished by the next day morning and dragged myself to Juliet. I asked, "Hey, could you distribute these for me? I need some sleep."

"Sure, Ella."

"Thanks."

She took the bracelets and ran off. I went to bed, hoping for a peaceful night, with no Malvagita running around, but of course, I was wrong.

In the dream, I was in a time that was probably much before now, as the land was full of trees and grass. I looked down and almost shouted in surprise. I was wearing an old fashioned dress and some weird jewelry. I checked my right hand, and there was an amulet, no, *My Amulet.* I yelped as I heard Estre's voice.

Generally, I am in your body. Now, you are partially in my body. Watch, but do not interfere. O.K?

Okay.

A couple of kids ran up and told her, "The great prophecy may be mistaken. War may not break out now. They must be waiting for one of us to leave."

"Prophesies are never mistaken, Amy Elementa. This one was given when I rose to be the first magician. Prophecies given at a new beginning always come true."

"Okay, Okay. What do you suggest we do?"

"We can -"

BOOM!!!

"Camp!" Cried the third girl.

"RUN!!!"

The three girls raced to the top of the hill overlooking the camp. They formed a little circle and touched each other's fingertips. Then they shut their eyes and concentrated. They started chanting, softly at first, but by the time they had finished, they had the undivided attention of the whole camp. They basically banished Malvagita for his evilness and unbalancing the magic, and sent him away until the magic became balanced.

Malvagita Ubella? He can't be here still, then!

We did a tiny error, Ella. We did not banish his apprentice. He is who has been causing all this mischief now. He has been helping us to achieve the balance. He has had many apprentices over the years, and every time, the speed increased.

So we must stop balancing?

NO!!

Then what?

We must prepare to fight. There needs to be a guard at every single place of discussion. Make sure nothing happens to the leaders. Now, Wake!

I woke up with a start and struck up a conversation with Estre.

Hey, did you really show me all that?

Yup.

Should I tell Juliet?

Yup. In fact, tell all the leaders left here. Malvagita wants only leaders. Move!

Okay, Okay, I'm up.

I got dressed and then ran up to Juliet. "Can – we – have – a – meeting – now?" I asked, trying to catch my breath at the same time.

"O.K. Now calm down and tell me what happened."

"Tell you in the meeting. Only the leaders that are remaining."

"What about the other Elements?"

I considered this. "The… the second in command."

"O.K."

Five minutes later, I found myself addressing a gathering of fourteen people, the fourteenth being me. I tried not to rouse panic, but it was kind of hard. When I finished, leaving out the part where Estre and her friends were chanting, the whole crowd started screaming. Even Juliet seemed flabbergasted. I said, "Ruhe!" Silent! Everybody fell silent. "Thank you. Now those who want to ask questions, please raise your hands."

Everybody raised his or her hands. I Pointed at one girl seated at my right and said, "Sie können sprechen." You may speak.

"Thanks," she said. "My name is Luna Mond. You said that we must not tell the others what exactly is going on. Why?"

"Because if we do, it will create mass panic. Next?"

It went on like this for a long time. Finally, I asked them, "Do you guys have combined practice any time? When, usually?"

"We have it once a month when a war is coming," Said a girl. *Teire,* I remembered. "It is kind of like a war game.'

"Well, that is not enough. From now on, we will have it once in two weeks. Juliet and I will decide when and we will let you know the morning of the Practice, and we will have it in the evening. Juliet, anything to add?"

"Nope. Meeting Adjourned. Go off now, and decide your teams. We will join too, but it may or may not be the way you think it is. Go!"

They left, talking excitedly about the game to come. After they left, Juliet asked, "Isn't once in two weeks a kind of overkill?"

"No," I said. "I left out a part." I told her about how exactly the dark magic was sent away, and she was shocked.

"So the problem is here now because the magic is being balanced?"

"Yup."

"Okay, so now, we have to have a practice as soon as possible. When is that?"

I smiled. "As soon as they give the names of the teams."

Chapter 8

It turned out that the practice games were a really popular idea. We got the teams the very next day, with team A being Earth, Water, Plants, Sun, Rainbow, and Animals, and team B being Fire, Air, Flower, Moon, Gems, and Stars. Juliet and I decided to be part of neither team, just run around and create general mayhem in the existing mayhem.The next day, we were standing in the middle of the crowd, and trying to pacify the people. Finally, I Silenced them.

"Okay, people! Rules: No using beads, except air in team B, since they do not have a Fire! So, he can use only the fire bead. No killing or wounding, except minor injuries. So, the game ends when one team has captured all the people in the other. Go to your positions!" They scrambled around. I removed the Silence, and then started the game.

As soon as everybody took their eyes of me, I muttered, "Niemand sieht mich, es sei denn ich sie zu wünsche." Let nobody see me unless I require it. I looked down, and turned invisible. I smiled. This would be fun.

As I wove in and out of crowds, I saw Juliet swirling a tornado to cause major confusion. I Jumped up and flew into it, taking it out of her control. She seemed surprised, and then smiled. She made two balls of fire and water, and shouted, "Mergere!" Merge! And it became one ball. She threw it at a bunch of fighting people, and said, "Bloccaggio." The ball transformed into a cage, and it captured the crowd. Then it split into two, taking the A team away from the B team.

I went after shrinking the tornado, and reached the place where the B team kept the A team captive. I threw the tornado and It sucked and kept captive the B team Guards. Then I Released the A team people, but they got sucked into the tornado too. Then I Split the tornado like Juliet, and threw some fiery snakes that prevented them from escaping. I then made sure that if someone stopped one tornado, then the other would also stop. I sent the tornado so high, that only a Wind guy could get it.

I Went to Juliet, and found her having a hard time with Water and Earth. I sent some vines to capture Earth, and encased Water in a miniature sun. She tried to put out the flames, but the water just evaporated.

"Argh! Get me out of here! Sun! You are in my team! Help me!" A blue message shot up in the sky. I quickly summoned some wind and tore it apart. I Sent another message. "Never mind. I am fine."

"What the-" She said, confused. Then she said, "Oh. Ella. Let me out, will you?"

"You should be more careful," I told her, and then sent her up along with the others. I then ran back to the thick of the battle. I found several people floating around, captured. I saw Air flying to free his companions with a Sun guy and a Plant guy. *Not so fast,* I thought. I captured the three of them and Sent them up too.

I saw a dark shape Flying towards the Stars girl who Juliet had captured. I realized that, as usual, nobody could see it except me. I flew forward and looked into its hood. "Cattiva Mauvais. Leave."

"How can you see me?"

"How can *you* see *me*?"

"Oh, I see."

"Same Invisible spell. That won't help you. I won't let you get them!"

Cattiva threw a spell at me and instinctively I raised a wall of flames to deflect it. He staggered behind, surprised. I chose that moment to summon a diamond and throw it at him. "Engraceleo!" Enlarge! I shouted. It enlarged and made to cut him, but he screamed, "Eclat!" Break! The diamond shattered into a million pieces. He collected it in a strong wind and flung them back at me. I raised a shield and they rained back on him. A few managed to cut his hands.

"Argh! I will get you for that, Ella!" By then, everybody noticed the blood dripping from his hands, and had muttered an anti-invisibility spell. Suddenly, he summoned a Ruby and flung it at me. I Shrunk it to the size of a bullet. At that precise moment, Malvagita appeared and sent some vines curling towards me. A boy Screamed, "No!" And sent the vines back to Malvagita. He set fire to them and sent it down. It Captured Juliet and the others. When he did that, I threw the ruby back at him. He had already Erected a shield, and it came back to me. I Sent it down and sent a stream of water along with it. When I did that, he yelled, "Bloccaggio!" I was captured. He lost no time in flying Towards the Stars girl. By then Juliet had been freed and she Flew up to stop them, but it was too late. In a flash of blinding light, Stella was gone, and so were Cattiva and Malvagita.

Juliet came and freed me, and then took me to the infirmary there. "Rest," she said. "You have done a remarkable amount of magic."

I was too tired to even protest. The moment my head touched the pillow, I slept.

Chapter 9

That night, I finally got to speak with Estre face to face. 'Course, it was only in a dream, but it was enough.

So, anyhow, As soon as I fell asleep, the image of Estre came into my mind's eye. "Hello, Ella. It's nice to see you face-to-face, one on one, finally. Sit down, and let us talk. I think some thing is bothering you?"

"Yes, Estre. First of all, how are you still in this world? Weren't you supposed to die long ago, like, five hundred years ago?"

"Yes, I guess I was. But Back then, people used to live longer, probably because the air was fresher. My brethren are also alive, but like me, they need a host, and unlike me, they need a willing host. So, we need to ask an non leader if they're willing to host Amy and Tiers."

"Is that all? How is Malvagita alive and in this world even without a host?"

"Well, we need to ask another non-leader. And it is my belief that if any kind of first magician can stay forever, as long as they have an apprentice, or are an apprentice. Okay?"

"Why non leaders?"

"Because Malvagita wants leaders. They will be captured, and so Amy and Tiers will be captured too."

"Okay. Any thing else?"

"Nope. Wake up, now."

I woke up with a start. I checked the time on a nearby clock, and told Estre, *So, Should I tell Juliet?*

No. Ask a stars girl for Amy, and a plant girl for Tiers. In the actual war, they will be your second in command. Okay?

Gotcha.

I ran to the stars place and found a girl weaving a starry sky above her. "Hey. Can I talk to you for a minute?"

"Sure, Ella. One sec."

She made to move her sky thing, but I waved my hand. It seemed to fold and it put itself in the girl's hand. In the Background, A voice yelled, "Cielo Estrella! Will you or will you not come inside?"

I yelled back, "She'll come in a few of minutes. Stay put."

"Ok."

"Come on out, Cielo."

Hey, Estre, Shields on?

Now it is. Tell her, Will you be willing to host one of the Second Elementas? She needs a willing host.

"Will you be willing to host one of the Second Elementas? She needs a willing host."

"Amy Elementa!?! Definitely!"

Take her to the entrance of Elementa's house and tell her to invite Amy inside her.

"Come on, then," I told her, and did as Estre said.

"She's in me!! It feels awesome!"

"Now, Cielo, do not tell anybody about the hosting. Do only starry magic. Do not tell anybody about it. You are the secret weapon. Go home, now."

"Thanks!"

I went and did the same process for a plant girl called Pianta Jeune. Then I collapsed on my bed, exhausted.

"Ella! Where have you been? I have been looking for you for half an hour!"

What do I tell Juliet?

Tell her that you went on a side project. Tell her that you cannot tell her.

I did that, and Juliet seemed to understand. She said, "We need to do dueling lessons now. Come on."

"Right now?" I asked. "Like, immediately?"

"Yes. Get your amulet charged. Charge it every day now. You cannot afford to run out of energy now."

"Okay, Okay, I'm up."

I went and got the amulet charged. Fortunately, neither Malvagita nor any other kind of Ubella, nor any Mauvaise came to capture anybody. I ran back and found a note. It said,

Hey, Ella. I'll be in a place where everybody is, yet is not. Find me...

Any idea where that is?

Yup.

Can you tell me?

Nope.

Not very helpful.

I know, but this is your first test.

Humph.

Okay, so the place where everybody is... that would be the cabins, but there were still a few people there... or the Meeting place! Nobody would be there now!

I ran to the meeting place. Nobody was there, which I found weird. I thought I saw a shimmer somewhere, and I turned. It was from the direction of the Charging place, but the shimmer had disappeared. I concentrated a little harder, and saw the Shimmers and everything, and I knew that they were there. I flew here to save time, and muttered an invisibility spell. Everybody shimmered to visibility. I spotted Juliet, Who said, "Well done. You are the fastest so far."

"Thanks. Wait, The fastest so far? You mean that every body does this?"

"Yup."

"Okay, so you were saying something about duel training?"

"Yup, Let us go to the auditorium, people!"

We all ran madly towards the auditorium. I found Pianta and Cielo. I warned them again and we went to the auditorium. Juliet yelled, "Who is first?"

"Me." A boy with a plant brooch stepped forward. Chaos died down. I heard some one whisper, "I wonder how she'll do. Arbre has been defeated only once!"

I started forming plans in my mind. I will be able to turn whatever he sends to me back. I decided to dry and burn the vines he sends me and send those to capture him. Then I remembered he had been defeated only once. I thought Juliet might have done the same thing. I decided to plan along the way.

BANG!!! The duel had begun. Immediately, he sent a vine that kept growing. I deflected it and changed it into a tornado. He took one of the empty beads I had given him and sucked in the storm. He threw it at me. I got it back into my amulet. Then he threw a fire bead at me. I took it into one of my empty beads and sent it back at him. He threw a water bead at it and it extinguished.

Use whatever I have. Hmm...

I summoned a leopard a few yards away. I concentrated a bit, and it turned and leapt at Arbre. Immediately, he tried to capture it and stuff.

At that precise moment, I sent a fire and water cage to captured him. He tried to send some vines out, but the fire burnt it.

For a moment, there was stunned silence. Then, everybody started cheering. Even Arbre smiled and said, "Well done, Ella! You are the second to defeat me! And the fastest so far. Let me out now?"

"Here."

He came out and gave me a pat on the back. "Brilliant! So, who's next?"

"Me."

Cielo stepped out of the shadows. I flashed her a warning message silently, and hoped she understood.

Bang!

The first thing she did was to throw her night sky at me.

"Metatroph!" Change! I turned it into a million birds and sent them pecking her. She threw her animal bead and they all fluttered towards it. I sent a ball containing all the four Elements, and at the same time, I sent a tiny, unnoticeable, 'sun' in the side. She ducked the big ball of Elements, and sent a wind, using the wind bead, propelling the ball towards me. I made it burst in a mini explosion, and she lost her balance and fell. The 'sun', which was hovering behind her, now expanded and covered her. "Bloccaggio!" I yelled. The 'sun' captured her. It stayed that way for five seconds, and then I said, "Freigabe." I helped her up and then asked, "Is anyone else coming?"

"Yes, but you are not going to use magic. No beads, no amulet. A sword. Arrows. Dagger. Those stuff."

"Fine."

She handed me a sword with a two feet long blade, and threw a spell at me. I reacted instinctively, and deflected it back to her. Then, she and Luna sent spells and beads in a rapid-fire action. Fire charred the blade, so I used the hilt. Juliet sent another fireball, and I got it in my blade. They backed me up to the wall, and I then released the fire that had been absorbed by the blade. I looked up, and the first thing I saw was a black shape shimmering in black mist. I looked carefully, and saw Malvagita and Cattiva. I threw my blade at Malvagita, and it pinned him to the wall by his sleeve. I pointed at him and shouted, "Bloccaggio!" And sent an Elemental ball at him, while throwing beads at Cattiva. People obviously noticed. I found Pianta and Cielo near me and told them, "Do not use any magic apart from your own branch and the common magic. They will know then."

"'Kay."

I dodged a water ball, and found a bow and a lot of arrows. I grabbed them, and sent arrow after arrow, until Cattiva was near his master. I was about to yell capture, when Cattiva screamed, "Freigabe!!!"

Malvagita was freed, and, faster than anybody could react; they sent a black mist towards us. It blew us all away, but two people remained – Arbre, and Fleur. It lifted them up, and then the four of them disappeared in a flash of light. Two more were captured.

Chapter 10

That night was miserable. There were only six leaders left, and even they were finding it more and more difficult to do magic. It was easier for Juliet and I as we were kind of like co-leaders. I felt furious, as those two sorcerers had captured my best friend, and the best dueler we all had.

I went and talked to Juliet, and we decided to go on with our usual activities, as it was impossible to stop them from entering. We told the other leaders to stay together at all times, and entered our quarters. We spent the rest of the night planning the defenses of the camp.

The next morning, we went to the training area again, and did some invisibility spells, and anti invisibility spells.

"*Ella!!!* Are you paying attention!?!" Juliet burst through my thoughts.

"No, can you repeat what you said last?"

Juliet rolled her eyes. I felt like doing that too, but I contained myself, and thought, *why can't she control herself?*

"I said, the phrase varies for each anti invisibility spell if you want to be precise, but there is one which you can use just about anywhere. Any guesses? And no helping, Estre."

"Riveli?"

"Riveli voi stessi."

"Can I try it?"

"No."

"Because…?"

"It is hard enough to perform magic as it is, without us having to waste some of it."

"All right."

"By the way, we need to keep another war practice soon. When?"

"Tomorrow. Let no one know."

"Cool. We will be?"

"You red, me blue."

"Done."

"By the way, it may seem irrelevant, but who was the first one to defeat Arbre?"

"Any guesses?"

"You?"

"Nope. Pianta."

"What!!"

"Are you surprised that Pianta won?"

"No, I am surprised that you lost."

"I'll take it as a complement."

"Take it as you wish."

We left the training area, and came face to face with Pianta and Cielo.

"Hey, Ella, can we talk to you for a second?"

"Sure. Catch up with you later, Juliet?"

"Okay."

I went to a little nook that I had found earlier that day, and made sure nobody could eavesdrop. I turned to them and asked, "So, what is it?"

"Amy and Tiers want to talk to Estre."

"Okay... Hold on."

Well?

Let me take over for 10 minutes.

What!!!

I swear that I will relinquish control after 10 minutes.

You could be lying. No offence.

None taken. You can weave a spell for this.

How?

Use my knowledge. Tell the other two now.

I did just that and waited. Suddenly, a flood of memories that were most certainly not mine entered my mind. It came with so much force that I nearly fell. I wove my spell from Estre's memories, and vaguely heard the other two doing just that. Suddenly, I seemed to have lost control over my body. I could say nothing, and feel nothing. I could only hear what was being said, but I could not say anything.

After exactly 10 minutes, I felt control coming back to me. I could feel Estre's reluctance to relinquish control, and nearly agreed to do that, but stopped. It would do us no good. I opened my eyes, and saw, for just one second, Tiers and Amy, but the next second, I saw Pianta and Cielo. By common assent, we left the place and went to our quarters.

Chapter 11

The next day, we decided to have another round of war games. Juliet and I shuffled the teams, with the red team with Plant, Star, Sun, Rainbow, Earth, Fire, and me. Our opponents, the clichéd blue team, were Animals, Flower, Moon, Gems, Water, Air, and Juliet. It was an even match, I guess, but Juliet had more experience.

That evening, I announced the rules of the game.

"Okay, people. This is a little different. We will play two rounds of this one. One person in each Element will be a captive, a prisoner. They can do nothing apart from what the defenses allow. So, the defensive team must be prepared for anything that will be thrown at you. The rest of the offensive team must attempt to rescue their fellow mates. You will have three hours to do this. Who goes first will be decided by the toss."

I picked up a coin that was blue on one side and red on the other. I threw it, and it came down and landed, showing the... "Blue team! Defensive! Red Offensive! Let the games begin! Oh, and by the way, the Team must capture the people; they will not be willingly given. Go!!"\

We ran to the red part, and I started putting up defenses around the strongest spell casters. I started doing it for myself when-

"I GOT HER!!! Come on, people! I got her!"

Oh no you don't... I thought. I felt a suffocating feeling on my chest, and I said, "Rendalo incosciente e fermi la sua magia!" Make whoever is using magic against me unconscious. This spell cannot be done by many people, as it required a lot of power. The pressure stopped, and I captured him. It was Steen. I placed defenses around me, and placed spells on him to make him tell the whole truth. I asked him, "What defenses are being placed around the place for the captives?"

"The usual types. No magic, no voice, no amulets, extra capture stuff, air tricks, tornados, and... yeah. That's about it. That I know of, at least."

"MMMPH!!!!"

I whirled around, and saw Juliet capturing Pianta. I freed Pianta, and we managed to get Juliet captured. I whispered a spell that prevented her and all those that were helping her from using magic, even beads, unless something Dark attacked. I heard several surprised cries that came from deep in the forest. Then, with no warning, I saw something silver flashing towards me. I sidestepped, and saw Luna with a dagger, coming again. I dodged, and stopped near Cielo. She said, "Her weapons are enchanted. No magic can stop them, and no magic can stop her while she holds it."

"I'll just have to do it the old fashioned way, then." I said grimly.

I took the sword that was hanging from one of my teammate's belts, Gabriel, and saw her draw her bow. I told her to keep Luna distracted, and I set about enchanting the weapon. When I was done, I saw Luna shoot an arrow towards Pianta. It seemed to root her to the spot. I freed her, and attacked Luna. She was fast. I managed to disarm her, but she just smiled. Before I could even take a breath to say the word for capture, she turned into water. I saw several others turn into water, but the people whom we had captured didn't.

I turned to Juliet and placed the spell that I placed on Steen on her. Then I asked her, "What are the spells that have been placed around the captives that Steen does not know of?"

"No beads," she said, as though she couldn't help it. "Whirlpools, Gems meant for capture, shooting weapons, and the other usual defense strategy."

"Is the no beads, no magic, no voice and no amulets for all or is it only for captured?"

"Only for captured."

I yelled at the rest of the team, "Let's go! We have to Get the rest of them! Go!"

We ran haphazardly at them, but we ran in such a way that our numbers seemed large.

Contact the leaders in your group.

What!? How?

I put an undetectable spell that will enable you to contact the leaders on the beads. Reach out with your mind.

Puzzled, I did that, but at first I felt nothing. Then, I felt the mind of a person whose mind seemed like the earth, fresh and sweet, but with a little bit of a short temper. I thought, *Gabriel?*

I felt a sense of panic radiating from her, and immediately said, *Calm down; it's just me, Ella.*

What?

Come to me. Our power is greatest when we are together.

Why?

We both are leaders. Well, not me, Exactly, but I hold enough power to be called one.

Is that why you & Juliet find it easier to do magic?

Yes.

I'll come.

The earth next to me trembled and formed a roughly humanoid figure holding a globe. The humanoid figure morphed into Gabriel. "Hey! I know that the earth is awesome for recharging, but isn't there another way to recharge? You can make a smaller model of the earth using your earth powers."

"I think I'll try that after this round. Thanks for the hint."

"Your welcome. Let's Go, shall we?"

"With pleasure."

This time, We were able to easily conquer the opponents, until…

"Well, looks like we have a combined deal, right boys?" a voice that sounded none too friendly sounded from behind. Then, there was a sword tip at my throat, and two arrows pointed at Gabriel. "Here, look at our champion dueler, the one who defeated Arbre Jeune, the one who *nearly* defeated the two Dark magicians herself, now held at a sword point." It was Teire.

"There is a difference. We both know that you wouldn't do it."

"What?"

"Wound me badly."

"Try me."

"With pleasure."

So saying, I stepped back and drew my sword. She looked surprised. I said "You have to always secure the back of your prisoner's body with a sword and his/her front with either a sword, another weapon, or your own body, in order to ensure that they do not escape. You ought to know that."

"I didn't expect you to know that. Most react differently to such a situation. They usually-"

I cut her short by lunging so fast that she could not follow, and gave her a small cut on her arm. She dropped her sword in surprise, and tried to run. I shouted, "Bloccaggio!" I Sent her to the place where the prisoners were kept.

"SURRENDER!!!"

I whirled around and saw about 10 people with their weapons ready, and some of them with the beads. "No way."

About 10 beads flew at me at once, none of them the earth ones, and erupted into their powers at once. I threw my entire bracelet of blank beads, while grabbing two. They all shimmered onto the other one, and my own refilled and came back onto my hand. I flicked my hand, and 20 beads flew off my hand, each person getting suppressed by two. All of them too became prisoners.

I turned to Gabriel, who seemed to have frozen on the spot. I realized that the two other leaders had not left. They were just stunned (with awe, it seemed). I changed that. I went into her mind, and told her what to do. We slowly overcame them, thanks to my extra power.

We continued in this fashion, until we reached the blue team's place. We sent a message to the others by a little communication system set up by Gabriel (I didn't understand a word of what she said about making it), and planned our strategy. We had to separate; but we still had magic a little more powerful than usual.

I messed up at once. As soon as she had gone, there was a guy with full armor, even for the hands, and he placed his weapon, some thing that felt like a sickle, around my neck.

"If you move back, you will hit the protruding's in my body armor. If you move to the sides, you will hit those in my arms. If you move forward, you will cut your own neck."

"Who are you?"

"Fiore Bluma."

I misheard him, and I asked, "Sorry, Fleur?"

"No! Fiore. F-I-O-R-E."

"Oh. Sorry. Well, Fiore-"

"Turn around."

I started doing that, when I heard the twang of a bow. Fiore spread his arms, and I saw and arrow on his arm. There was Pianta, standing with a bow in hand, saying, "That will not be a grievous wound, Fiore."

"Very funny, Pianta. But I take it that this has no poison?"

"No, but you will sleep for the next two hours."

As soon as she said this, Fiore started losing consciousness. In the next second, he was snoring.

"Let's go, shall we?"

"Yeah. Thanks."

I asked after some time, "Not a grievous wound?"

She smiled and said, "Inside joke."

We moved along the paths decided by us. I, as planned, went behind the guard in the back, and after contacting Gabriel, made a twig grow, and stepped in it. It made a loud crack, and the guards heard me. They were an animal guy and a stones girl. I went as though I hadn't heard them, and She threw a stone at me. When it as an inch away from me, she said, muttered something.

The stone touched me, and I found myself in front of Luna Mond. She was seated on a small stool, in a little fortress sort of a thing. She said, "Hi! Got you back, didn't I?"

"I guess."

I was carted back to the prisoners' area. I carefully memorized the way, and waited until their footsteps receded. Then I turned to the others in the cell. I did a headcount, and there were six people apart from me, Cielo included. I silently cursed. I then did the communication system thing. This didn't require any magic, so that was safe. Cielo didn't realize this, and so I told her what had to be done in sign language, as there was a no voice rule. I contacted Gabriel and Pianta, and told them everything that I saw. I also told them to bring some 50 people, so as to easily overwhelm them. And then I waited.

And waited.

And waited.

Suddenly –

Thud.

Thud.

Thud.

There was a sudden roar, then a burst of light. The spells placed on us were gone, and I led the charge out. I joined Gabriel and took Cielo along with me, and we shouted, "We won!!!!"

Then all the magic that was done in the duration of the game was undone, and the other people came there. We switched sides, and decided to do the reverse game another time.

Chapter 12

We all started the daily activities a little late, having overslept. We charged the amulets, and the leaders, co-leaders and Replacement leaders came to the auditorium to practice together. We did things like one on one, two on one, and so on. After that, we went to the ground. I ran into Apprendista, unexpectedly. "Can we talk?"

"Sure."

She pulled me into a little hiding place sort of a thing, and said, "I had a dream last night."

"Why tell me?"

"It regards you, and the upcoming war."

"Hold on." I just put an anti eavesdropping spell around us, and then said, "Continue."

"You and Juliet Changed places. I Know that much, and that is enough. I had a vision about the war. I saw You dueling Malvagita and Cattiva. The others were going against the army of shadows. Oh, and Pianta and Cielo were trying to go to the leaders."

"What about the leaders?"

"They seemed to be struggling against something invisible. Their amulets were getting charged perpetually. Here's the peculiar thing.

Malvagita didn't seemed to be losing any energy, but you and Cattiva were exhausted. Any ideas why?"

"Not yet. But I hope you understand why these memories must be wiped out of your mind?"

"Absolutely."

I did that, and then left with her. I went to Juliet and told her that her memories of the swapping day had to be wiped, and did that before she could protest, such that If the need arises, I could invoke that memory, and become a leader or co-leader depending on the necessity.

I decided to consult Estre on the duels matter, and held a rather long mental conversation with her.

Well? I said.

The first part is obvious. They somehow find out about the swap, and duel you.

How could they have?

Maybe you decide that the best time to declare leadership is then. Maybe they capture both you and Juliet at the same time. But whatever be the case, you must increase the defenses about the Balance, by maintaining the balance in camp, and by putting a balanced defense around camp borders.

I understood about half of that, but fine. But why was Malvagita not getting tired at all?

Maybe he will join the duel when you and Cattiva both exhaust yourselves.

But the amulets-

That may have been a mistake. The chargers may have been kept for Cattiva and Malvagita's amulets.

But they wouldn't make such a silly mistake.

Malvagita never won any of the wars he waged for that very reason.

That is to our advantage, I hope?

Yes. Now rest. We need to do a lot of work tomorrow.

All right. But I will keep questioning you tomorrow.

Fine. Good night.

Good night.

Chapter 13

The next day, we started early. We needed to use the dark magic on purpose this time, so of course, we all were nervous. What we were doing was unprecedented, so there was no proof that it would actually work. The marks of the defenses are there even today. The mark- wait. Let me tell you the whole thing.

We started planning, and this time, a part of Estre was there too. We had just started to plan when we heard a bit of thunder. Estre stood up, alarmed.

"Calm down. It is just a bit of thunder." said someone.

Estre fired up at once. "Do you even know what that thunder is? I'll tell you. A Dark apprentice, but not Cattiva, sent that. Yes, there must be another. Either Malvagita has two, or there is another Dark magician. Let us hope it is nothing, but Dark thunder is the first thing that a dark apprentice is expected to summon."

"How do you Know this?"

"I Know because I was, for a very short period of time, Captured by the one who is threatening us now."

"Can't Cattiva have summoned it later during his apprenticeship?"

"No. There is only one Kind of starter thunder. It cannot be so, unless... Of Course!! Cattiva and Malvagita must have been together for 14 years now, and this must be the beginning of their 15th year. Therefore, their bond will not be as strong as they were at first. They have to renew their bond. We have about a month before their next attack, if they wish to have the same kind of efficiency."

"Is it possible for us to attack them?"

"Yes, but that is not advisable. We require all the leaders, so either we get back all the leaders, or we wait until all the leaders are captured, and then the attack will be perfect, and we will have a chance of winning."

"Why doesn't Juliet or Ella take an apprentice by then?"

"They have their reasons."

Then some lightning hit the entrance to camp, and there was a clap of thunder that seemed to be charged with darkness. We all stepped out, together, so as to increase our power.

It was absolutely chaotic outside. Since the leaders were not present, the others were going round in confusion. Juliet shouted, "Defense Formation! Rally at the Rhea point! Go!"

"Fire is absent!"

"Fire, Water, swap! Ella, you are at the fire's spot. Leaders! Form the point!"

We ran to the required spot, and we made a formation like an arrow, and locked our right arms in front. Almost immediately, two black figures flew towards us on a black cloud. We raised our arms above us, but they just landed in front of us.

"Listen! We do no wish to attack. We just need something that You are keeping away from us."

"What is it that you require, Malvagita Ubella?"

"I require your ex-apprentice, Juliet Elementa. I need Apprendista Elementare."

"Why is that so, Ubella?"

"I am performing an experiment."

"What about the people that You and Your apprentice has snatched away from us?"

"They too are necessary for my experiment."

"Return them, and explain your experiment to the council. If we are unanimous for your cause, then we will allow Your experiment to proceed."

"The waiting can be no longer. Either give her to us willingly, or we will take her away by force."

"It is against our principles to give away our campers to a Dark magician without finding, and eliminating, the risk."

"Then the attack shall begin, and the one whom we want will come."

"As the ancient White ones will, so it shall be. The attack will be well defended. Think before you proceed."

"I have made up my mind. None can change my will."

"Then let us begin!"

Malvagita and Cattiva Flew over the lines, and we all raised our hands and brought them down. Somehow, I knew exactly what I must do. Malvagita and Cattiva flew towards us, and were thrown off track. Cattiva, furious, threw a black arrow at the nearest person, Apprendista. Suddenly, she was becoming smoke, and she stood there, Trying to put herself together. Someone threw a white arrow at her, but it went right through her. She became a complete smoke figure. She was sucked into a white butterfly amulet, like dirt into a vacuum cleaner, and Cattiva wore it on his left hand. Then they said unanimously, "Our mission successful, we depart, hoping to have accomplished something fruitful by this visit."

Before they left, Malvagita raised his hand. "Something to remember this by." Lightning struck the ground and charred it black.

They flew off, and we were absolutely disorganized. We hoped that the ones who were captured were safe, and that we could see them soon, though it may seem impossible...

Chapter 14

That night, I was absolutely exhausted, having put sufficient defenses to prevent an attack. I asked, "What is the Rhea point? I mean like, What is its significance?"

"It is the best place for defense."

"Explain."

"We can see the entire camp from two points, one is the Campers point, and the other is the Rhea point."

"The name comes from?"

"When we were sieged by Dark magicians for the second time, The Elementa leaders were Rhea and Meilleur, the latter the lead one. Well, Meilleur was almost killed, and she was in no condition to lead. She passed on her leadership to Rhea, and waited in the Elementa room. Rhea gathered the whole camp at that point, and placed a spell on that area that made the campers do everything in perfect coordination. The Dark side was vanquished, but when Rhea was dueling Malvagita, she got fatally injured. She threw all the dark creatures and people out of camp with one last spell. She died there. Hence the name, in the memory of Rhea Elementa."

"Oh."

After a moment, she said, "You know, the main question is, Why did they want Apprendista?"

"Really? I thought it was one of these- what is the experiment? What role does The Leaders play in this? How – never mind. The point is, there are so many questions, and none of them seem to have any answers right now. The best thing we can do now is to train the people in defending attacks from other Elements."

"How?"

"How did Apprendista?"

"She did it by extreme concentration."

"Then we will make them do it by extreme concentration."

"Should we call them to the auditorium now?"

"No. Say this – All Elements are requested to assemble at the place where we get what we need, whenever we want, without us doing anything."

"The-"

I clamped my hand over her mouth. She looked at me in surprise, and then relaxed. "Mmph, mph-mmph..." Translation- I get it. Let my mouth go now, or else...

I took my hand of her mouth. "Thank you. Now, Will you do the honors?"

"Yeah." I said a spell that made my voice be heard in every corner of camp, but not beyond. Then-

"All campers! This is an important announcement! You are all requested to assemble at the place where we get what we need, whenever we want, without us doing anything but going there. I repeat, you are all requested to assemble at the place where we get what we need, whenever we want, without us doing anything but going there. Please come immediately. Please remember to put anti-spying spell on yourself before going there."

We, Juliet and I, went to the Charging area after putting on the anti-spying thing. While we were waiting, we charged our amulets to the limit. I also got some Stones magic onto a ring that I had worn. That gave me an advantage over others. Almost immediately after this, we heard footsteps. We looked at the entrance, and saw – Pianta and Cielo entering. Following them were Luna and Gabriel. Something seemed wrong. I then noticed what. I drew my sword, which I had decided to keep after the battle at Rhea point.

"Oh, I wouldn't do that if I were you," Said a soft voice from the shadows. Malvagita and Cattiva stepped out. "If you do, I will have no choice but to destroy her source of power." He gestured to Gabriel. I lowered my weapon and started to sheath it, when Malvagita said, "None of that. Slowly lower your weapons down, and then turn around, both of you, and put your hands to your side. Good, that is good. Gleichheit stark und schmerzlich." Mouth full, eh? It means tie rigidly and painfully.

So, I felt something bind me tightly, starting with my arms, and then doing my feet. Surprised, I fell down, and by the sounds of it, so did Juliet. Then, another one tied me down to the ground, with one placed such that if I tried to get up, I would get choked. It also seemed to be charged with dark magic. All these ropes were so tight, with the exception of the one around my neck, that it brought tears to my eyes. Cattiva came with two pieces of black cloth. He gagged us with it, first Juliet, then me. The moment the cloth touched me, I felt all the energy drain out from me, and my amulet drain itself.

"I will leave a mark of my visit this time too, for you seem to have forgotten me." Malvagita bent over both of us, First Juliet, then me, and traced the symbol of infinity onto my hand, and three short lines onto hers. The marks burned so much that I nearly blacked out, but I managed not to do that, though Juliet didn't. Cattiva traced a circle onto the hands of the four campers, and immediately, they collapsed.

Malvagita whispered to me, "This time, I will leave your campers be. Next time, there will be a little more chaos, which I am sure that you don't want. Remember, I have warned you." He summoned some lightning, and I blacked out.

Chapter 15

When I woke up, I was still lying down on the ground, still tied painfully tight, and still with something burning on my hand. The others were waking up too, but I didn't pay much attention to them. I tried gathering my strength, but there was none left. Gabriel and Pianta tried to get up, but by the sound of it, I guessed that they were tied up too. The others were still trying to recover from the shock. I tried to shout through the gag. I also tried to send a message to Gabriel, but it didn't work. I then gave three short shouts, followed by one long one. Juliet tried to shout through her gag, three short ones, and nodded at us, as much as she could with her neck position, and we shouted. It was reasonably loud, and then someone ran in from outside. It was Fiore.

"What on earth happened?" He asked as he untied us, First Juliet, then me, then Gabriel, then Luna, Then Pianta, and finally Cielo.

"Summon all the leaders here, Fiore. You may stay here too, as I want the replacement leaders here also." Juliet sounded so tired as she said this.

"Yes, Juliet." He left.

"Show me your arms, all of you. I need to check whether or not he has left a mark on your hands." We all extended our right arms towards her, and I saw that he had put small white marks in and around each of our tattoos.

"Three lines. He could not have given me a better way to remember each and every year I spent in camp. Did he give any of you a message?"

"Yeah. He told me, 'This time, I will leave your campers be. Next time, there will be a little more chaos, which I am sure that you don't want. Remember, I have warned you.' What he meant was obvious. What did he tell you?"

"Only something regarding the lines. It will increase in number, one for every year I spend here."

"He told me something," said Pianta. "He said two things. Firstly, that I was to tell you two that the next will be Teire, and two, that I seemed to be powerful, and so during the final war, he... He will have an army of shadows just for me."

"He has an Anima Tueur, a soul Slayer. I Saw it, with a capital S."

We all fell silent as we grasped the implications of what Luna said.

"And," said Cielo, breaking the silence. "He said that he could sense something different about us, something he couldn't pin point. Pianta and me. I dunno what he meant."

The last part was a lie. I knew it, and so did Pianta. But of course, we said nothing. Then Fiore came in with the leaders.

"Take this. Someone threw this on the wall of stones." He handed me my sword. "Will you explain what happened?"

"Yes, but is every body here?"

"All the leaders, sub leaders, and co leaders."

"OK. Juliet?"

"Let us begin the usual way this time."

Every single person uttered an anti dark spell under his or her breaths. Juliet indicated that I should do the same thing. I did that, and then I waited. The others seemed to take a long time to finish. I began to feel that I had missed something, but after they were done, she said, "Congratulations. You have been the most specific in the shortest period of time. Now, let the meeting commence."

We began by telling the others about the most recent attack by the two. Then we informed them about two things. "The next person to be captured is Teire. That you may feel is alarming, but listen to this. Malvagita has an Anima Tueur. This is the *worst* thing that can ever happen."

Do we need to tell them about the dream? I asked Estre.

NO!!! Was the immediate reply.

Okay, calm down. Can I go tell Juliet?

Never. You know why.

Yes.

"Any questions?"

"Yes. Are you going to give any extra protection to Teire?" That was Luna.

"No." I replied.

"Why not?" Asked Teire, somewhat hurt.

"Every time we try to give the leaders some extra protection, they fail. There is no way we are able to get around this problem. We are only wasting our energy."

"Isn't trial and error the best way to learn?"

"Not all the time. We need to, in this case, do something only when we are relatively sure about what is to be done, about what will actually work. Any other questions?" I made it clear that the rest of the answer is confidential, and that it is a big thing that we told them so much.

There were no more questions. I wonder why.

"I have one. How is it that Malvagita was able to get through our defenses so easily? Can anyone answer that?" Juliet's voice had a hard edge.

"Maybe I can." Estre materialized beside me. "He has a spy."

"No way. Impossible."

"Hah! He does that every time. He takes someone close to all of us, and then twists that person into believing his ways, or doing something else, but always converting them in the end. Now who could that be? We only started putting defenses around us after a few days after the third or fourth capture. Is it one of us? Is it one who is sitting here, putting on an expression of innocence, or outrage?"

Everybody squirmed uncomfortably under her gaze except three of us - Juliet, myself, and...Fiore.

Well?

Watch him.

Excuse me?

You heard me. Ask him later in an admiring sort of way.

Fine. But I do not think that it is him.

As you like him?

I froze. *I do not! I just can't Imagine Fleur's trusted friend doing something like this.*

"Ella!"

"Yeah?"

"Ideas?"

"Increase defenses for everything." I had another Idea, but I did not want to tell it to one and all.

"Define everything."

"Leaders, no wait, strike that. Sub leaders, Defense positions, offence positions, war games areas, recharge areas, and so on, and so forth."

"Common areas?"

"Yup."

"Let us begin.

Hey, Ella.

Malvagita!?!

Yes. The burn lets me speak to you. So, I Know your extremely awesome plan. Cool, huh?

Yeah right.

Good plan, but I already told my magician.

Can you talk to the others as well?

Certainly, but why bother, now that I have you?

I am flattered, I said, my voice dripping with sarcasm.

He was *amused.*

I put defenses around my mind while still talking, and then kicked him out. I decided to tell the others later.

Chapter 16

We began by putting the Defenses that none else knew about. Then, I broke the news about the 'burns for communication' to the others.

"When did you figure out?" Asked Juliet.

"In the middle of the meeting."

"Sooner for you, it seems. Anything else?"

"Have you put defenses to prevent this ridiculously easy walk in capture?"

"No. Be my guest."

"Translation: You won't help me?"

"Right."

"Fine. but why?"

"It's not like he would walk in and capture us."

Its best to be prepared, I thought. I designed something to incorporate all the things. Starting from the outer, it goes,

1. Flower shaped wall with five petals
2. At the tip of petal and joint of petal-stars
3. Water stream along the inside of the wall
4. Leaf shaped walls around the next wall for leaves

5. Flower shaped wall with flowers at each petal (Not literally)

6. Rainbow behind flower

7. Animal at flower Joint

8. Moon behind animal

9. Air between moons

10. Ring of fire

11. Ring of earth

12. Sun in center

So at each shift, we needed an earth, an air, a fire, a water, five plants, five flowers, one sun, five moons, ten stars, five animals, five rainbows and five stones. So, totally, forty people per shift.

I showed this to Juliet, and she was like, "This is fool proof! We have a total of one sixty campers, apart from the leaders, including you for the leaders, so that would mean four shifts, for six hours each."

When she paused for breath, our amulets began to glow, and Juliet said, "Cool, a new person. A girl, I hope. The boys are hopeless. They take too long to get used to camp."

We ran to the auditorium, but nobody was there. We then prepared the place for the new kid. We basically got the Amulets ready for selection, along with a few things for the dramatic effect. As soon as we were done, others started filing in. This time, Fiore set out to bring the person. It was a boy. I smiled at Juliet. "Hopes dashed?" I whispered. She shot me a look that said, '*Shut up.*'

"Hey, people. I'm Stren Majier."

"Welcome," Juliet said with a hard edge.

"Cool. What am I supposed to do?"

"Stay there until you are called." We had discussed this (argued, actually. I did not want to do It.). I moved my hand dramatically. The cloth covering the amulets moved away, and…nothing. I raised my eyebrows at Juliet. She muttered an anti dark spell, and then a curse. *They don't work here,* I realized. I then Gestured towards the ceiling, and then down came the Elementa amulet, and the Dark amulet. The floated towards my hand, and I held it forward. They both paused for a moment, and then, the Elementa one slowly floated towards him. Juliet and I winced. It tied itself to his hand, and he seemed to have had a vision too.

"Step forward, Stren Elementa. Hail."

"That's Stren Majier."

Everybody let out nervous laughs. "That," I said, "Is your birth Name. This is your power, or in this case, powers."

In my mind, I was thinking, *Why another?*

Chapter 17

I put a few anti-dark spells around us. We then had to walk Stren around camp. It was strenuous. Luckily, Juliet had it all planned, except for his awkward questions.

"So, basically, you just take some nature magicians and get them away from other nature magicians, and we're supposed to be the good side. Right?"

"God, Stren, you are supposed to be an Elementa. Please act like it." I chided him.

"So what's up with this Elementa stuff? The things there are so not Elements."

"Duh. But they are nature." Juliet said.

"Hmm."

"'Elementals' are the proper name for the 'nature magicians', as you so eloquently call them." Her voice was dripping with sarcasm at the last part. "Elementas have *all* powers. Earth, air, fire, water, plant, flower, sun, moon, stars, animals, rainbows, and precious stones."

"Twelve powers. Well, make that thirteen, 'cause I am awesome at arts."

"That is not magical." I said.

"Yes, it is, 'cause what I draw comes to life."

"Yeah right."

"Want proof?"

"If it is real."

"A stick or something, please."

I gave him something, and then he drew a puppy. The moment he finished drawing, It seemed to peel of the ground and grow, and became... a puppy.

"Cool. Anything else?" I said.

"No. Why?"

"There is a war going on, and we may find some use for your skills. So, anything else?"

"No. A *war?*"

"Yeah. There will be war every time there is More than one Elementa."

"A war since I came?"

"No, since I came."

Juliet and I held up our amulet hands. "Come on." I walked off with Juliet, and he followed, talking all the way, of course. I ignored him and conducted a mental conversation with Estre.

Well?

I thought he would be a stars magician, but he isn't.

I know. But what is your advice on the education of this guy?

You do it. Now.

Seriously?

Deadly.

Okay...

Begin!

That is like a duel begin... I said hesitantly.

Well, it is a good way of kick starting the magic.

What if his amulet is almost empty?

It isn't. Go!

Tell Juliet. I do not want her to interfere.

I will.

I told Juliet to go on without us, and then I Pulled Stren to the dueling area. It was empty.

We stood facing each other, and I attacked.

"Whoa! Hold your horses."

"Defend yourself!"

He dodged, and then kept muttering, "I need a stick." He thought for a moment, and I made something very near him burn. Then, the amulet glowed, and he raised his hand. Water spurted out of his arm. I diverted the flow after it doused the fire, and I put it in one of the empty beads. He grew a stick and started drawing something huge on the ground. I tried to blow the wind and distort the picture, but he stopped it. *Estre...*

Stop drawing, boy.

"Why should I? She attacked me."

That is how you must train.

"Oh yeah? Whoa!"

Estre materialized before him, and she did look a little dramatic, but she looked powerful. "It is necessary. You want to learn magic? We need to kick start it first."

"Oh. But couldn't you give me a warning?"

"No. Your mind would be prepared then."

"Okay."

Estre came back in me. *Thanks.* "Sorry." I said out loud. Can you come with me?"

"Fine." He huffed.

We walked a bit, and then I showed him my ground plan. "Can you build this by drawing it? It is a defense thing for around camp."

"Yes, but what material do you want?"

"Something hard to bend and break, even by magic. Anything to suggest?"

Lutetium Metal?

Say what?

Hardest metal on the entire planet. It's silvery white corrosion-resistant.

"Estre says Lutetium metal. Silvery white corrosion-resistant metal."

"I can do that. I've seen pictures of it. Who's Estre?"

"That lady who convinced you to stop drawing."

He grew a stick, and redrew my ground plan, except a bit more perfect. He said, "Three...two...one...Go!"

The ground began to rumble, and the walls began to raise themselves, and it was made up of a metal. I ran up to the walls and made sure nobody was on top of the wall (the ultimate example of wrong place, wrong time). I pulled the water bead that I had just filled, and threw it at the water area. It filled itself with water. I went to the auditorium and called everybody there. I made the leaders sit separately.

"Okay, people, you may have noticed the walls and things here. I have just got them built, and they are for defense. We need a total of forty campers per shift. One earth, one air, one fire, one water, five plants, five flowers, one sun, five moons, ten stars, five animals, and five gems. We will have four shifts of six hours each, starting from twelve midnight, and going round the clock. We three will also do this, but with eight hour shifts. Clear?"

"Yes, Ella." They chorused. I nearly smiled. "Anything to add?"

"Show them your plan?"

"Sure." I raised my hands and looked at Juliet. I made a model of the defenses with the Elements' symbols. I made some water freeze, and kept them as the walls. I got the same reaction from them as I had got from Juliet.

We got the shifts settled, and I sent Stren to his shift. And then we all slept, except those on the shift.

Chapter 18

I woke up at 12 in the morning and went for my shift. Nothing unusual had happened the previous night, and nothing happened during my shift except another Element's shift. I passed it on to Juliet and then I left to eat. Suddenly, Estre spoke.

Do you know what the unbreakable oath is?

No...

It's one in the oldest magical language.

Is it...

No, not the one you know.

Then?

Some letters flashed in my mind.

Great. Pronunciation please?

The way it is indicated.

Words?

Go to the ancient library-

There's a library here?

Ask Juliet.

I marched up to the center guard, and asked, "Hey, do you have a libr-"

"Later."

"It is important!"

"More than you think."

I felt Estre leave me partially. She said to us, *Do you agree to let us visit it?*

Yes. I heard Juliet's voice.

She came back. Estre then led me to a little room in the camp, and said, *There. Press your amulet on that mirror.*

What?

You heard me.

I did that, and then felt something like an electric shock there. I closed my eyes, and when I opened them, I was in a room that looked like a room in a palace. Red curtains were between the pillars, and here and there, an Elementa symbol was engraved on gold. I noticed several tall shelves closed with a golden door, and a carving that looked like the Elementa symbol, but it was like the amulet would fit in there perfectly. *Where do I look?*

Top shelf. Press your amulet on the groove, and say, PRIMA LINGUA. Remove your hand immediately after that. Now.

I did that, and I found that my suspicion was right. The door shimmered into non-existence, and a scroll with a royal purple seal floated down to me. I held it with both hands, and asked Estre, *Now what?*

She seemed tense. *Say Aperatur opera, operari elementorum.*

Meaning?

You will learn now.

I did that, and with a blinding flash of light, the seal disappeared, and laid itself on a table with a pair of spectacles on the side. The spectacles were like an adjustable power thing. I went and sat at the table, and looked at the scroll. It said...nothing. *What is this!*

Wear the glasses. There are thirteen pairs of lenses in the glasses. Go through them one by one. Once you are done with all of them, I'll tell you what to do before closing the scroll.

I first counted the lenses, and I realized that there were only six pairs. *Estre! There are only six pairs!*

WHAT!!!

She told me to go on reading, and I did. As I went on reading, I finished all six pairs. I decided to try combinations, and I discovered more to read. Estre came out of me and put it back to mode six. "Say Aliquam scientia revelante. Spero me retinere." Thank you for revealing this information to me. I hope you will let me keep it.

A deep voice boomed. "COME TO ME AFTER THE WAR, ELEMENTA...IF YOU ARE ALIVE."

Let's go. The leaving mirror is there.

I left, thinking about what I learnt.

As I left the library, my mind was buzzing with a lot of questions. I was about to ask Estre, but I needed to see her face. I went to the Elementa room, and told her to come out. She obliged.

"What happened in the library? Why do you want me to learn the language? Who was that person who told me to go back there and why did he? What happened to the other seven lenses? When -"

"STOP! Slow down. You understood what Custos Cartis said?"

"Yeah. Why is that surprising?"

"He said it in Prima Lingua."

"Okay. Why is that so amazing?"

"You didn't read the entire scroll! You read it through only six lenses! It shouldn't be possible!"

"Why didn't you let me read the combinations?"

"That is dangerous magic. I'll tell you about it later."

"Why not now?"

"You need to concentrate."

"Why do you want me to learn the language?"

"We can make the others swear oaths in that language. That will reduce the chances of spying, though…Oh no!"

"What?"

"Malvagita knows the language, and it's spells. We need to counter those."

"Meaning?"

She took a deep breath. "We need to go back there."

"Why are you so scared of the place?"

"Bad experiences."

"Elaborate."

"No." She came back in without waiting for a response. *You know what to do.*

I went back to the mirror, and to the library. Immediately, the voice said, "IS THE WAR OVER SO SOON?"

Estre came (out) to the rescue. "No, Custos. We need to know the information, if we need to defeat the Dark One."

"HE ROSE AGAIN?"

"He never died."

"SO YOU TOLD THE TRUTH."

"I said it in Prima Lingua."

"WHAT IS IT THAT YOU NEED?"

"Has he ever come here?"

"I CANNOT REVEAL INFORMATION TO ANYONE BUT THE MAKERS."

"I *am* a maker.'"

"SAY IT IN PRIMA LINGUA."

"Ego sum factorem."

"NO, HE HAS NEVER COME HERE."

"Where are the lenses?"

"WITH HIM."

"What has he done with them?"

"HE HAS ENCHANTED THEM SO THAT HE CAN READ THE DARK SPELLS IN THE BOOK."

"Ella, Get the scroll and read the ones that I had stopped you from reading."

I was about to place the Amulet on the groove, but Custos said, "I FIRST NEED YOUR WORD THAT YOU WILL COME TO ME AFTER THE WAR, IF YOU ARE ALIVE."

I glanced at Estre. She hesitated, and then nodded slightly. "Veniam ad vos post bellum, si vivo."

"GOOD." The scroll floated down to me. "YOU NEED NOT EVEN ASK. ESTRE TELLS ME WHAT YOU NEED, I GIVE YOU THE REQUIRED SCROLL."

"Sas Eucharisto." Thank you.

I went to the table with the scroll, and then I read. First, it was how to do simple spells. Then, it was how to counter simple spells from outside. Then it was how to counter simple spells in the other language, from the inside. Then, it was how to cast spells without speaking them. And so on, and so forth. In the last combination, the thirty-sixth, It disappeared. "SAY, IN PRIMA LINGUA, ALLOW ME TO SEE THE SPELLS, FOR THE KEEPER OF THE SCROLLS HAS TOLD ME TO DO SO."

"Liceat videre pertinet ad id ad me custodem in libris." Allow me to see the spells, for the keeper of the scrolls has told me to do so.

It shimmered and appeared. I read the spells, and was about to say the finishing line, when Custos said, "THE KNOWLEDGE WILL

REMAIN WITH YOU, AS LONG AS YOU REMEMBER THE LIBRARY."

"Thank you." Estre came back into me, and we left.

Well?

Let's do it.

Chapter 19

The first thing I noticed the moment I came out of the library was that Estre was tense, and was pushing against something. I looked for whatever it was, and guess what I found?

MALVAGITA.

Ella! Prima Lingua!

Hinc sunt te ac complices tuos animo meo expulsus! Cedamus! Basically, It means, you and your accomplices will get out of my mind. Surrender.

Protegamur! Protect.

His shield, though rather rough, prevented my spell from taking effect. I felt another mind, not as powerful, but easily detectable. It took a solid form, and I saw Cattiva. My mind partially took a solid form, leaving the rest of it protecting important information. Cattiva (I'm using his name for his mind, so don't get confused) Drew his sword, and I drew mine. He came in fast, and I realized from my reading that he couldn't use magic. I quickly blocked a blow, and we went edge on edge. I thought, *Augeret potestate mea!* Increase my power. I Felt stronger, and thrust my sword forward. He blocked me, and I twisted my blade, catching his cross-guard above my blade. He tried to withdraw, but I spun my sword in a circle, and nicked him in the arm, before catching his hilt. I twisted, and the sword went flying beyond his head. I tried to stab him, but he retreated from my mind. I then took this form of mine, and went to help Estre.

She needed it.

She was so exhausted, that if she had a body, she would have collapsed. She seemed to be locked in a battle that she couldn't move away from. I looked over to Malvagita.

He was not the least tired. In fact, he seemed to be toying with her. He seemed to have an endless supply of energy.

I did the sensible thing. I joined the fray, after whispering a spell. *Crescite potentia de me et sociusque!* Increase the power of my ally and myself.

I came in, after my power increased by tenfold. Estre seemed to have grown stronger too. Malvagita seemed to notice me, and he solidified. He glided through Estre, and I was all that stood between him and my memories. He pulled a black sword that had a platinum strip in the middle. It seemed to glow. I raised my sword, which had the perfect ratio. I raised my sword, and he attacked. He came in point first, and I thought how nice it would be if my mind self had armor made of lutetium. I got the armor, and it was rather light. I raised my sword and blocked the first bow, simultaneously summoning another sword. I then went in, still having a constant supply of energy. Malvagita seemed to be quite serious, and he gave me a cut on my main sword arm. I felt Estre reinforce the protection around my mind. He came in with an attack that required a lot of force, and I caught it on my blade. I then kept him in lock, and kept my other sword about five inches above that. I pulled above, and the sword came free of his hand and landed in the ground before me. I kicked it aside, and hit him with the sword. Needless to say, he withdrew too.

I made some reinforcements to my mind's protections, and retreated into my mind. Only then did I realize that my eyes had been closed, and Stren was leaning over me with a worried expression on his face. "What happened?" He said, after hastily (and poorly) disguising the look on his face.

"Nothing. Why do you ask?"

"You kind o' collapsed after you got in this room. I happened to be passin' by at that time, and I came in and tried to wake you up."

I realized two things at that moment. One, I was in a toolshed sort of thing. Two, I was clutching my arm at the exact same place where Malvagita cut me. I slowly let go, and got up. I felt weakish, and the place where I cut my mind self hurt. As soon as I got up, Stren said, "You've got a cut in your arm, and that was definitely not there when I came in. What is going on?"

I looked there, and I saw that the cut was worse than it was in my mind self. Estre was worried.

"Good question. I have no idea about this cut, but I can tell you that there is a war going on."

"Explain."

"How about when we get to the Elementa room?"

"Sure, But you must explain, 'kay?"

"Word of honor."

"Good. I'll hold you on that promise."

We walked in silence, at least on the outside. I was asking Estre what to tell and what not to tell, and I bumped into Pianta and Cielo. "Hey guys. Sorry."

"We need to talk. Again."

"Stren, I'll meet you after this little talk. I'll explain then, Okay?"

"Okay."

I walked away, and Stren followed. "Stren, go to Juliet. I need to talk to these girls privately."

"Fine." He stalked off.

We went to a little place near the charging area. "Please do not tell me that they want to talk to Estre face to face again."

"No. It's just that…" This was Pianta.

"We both were attacked with minds. Malvagita and Cattiva."

"Me too."

"Well… He's found out about Amy and Tiers."

My blood went cold. "Are you sure?"

"Yes." Said Cielo. "He said, 'So, You've got this one, Amy, and Tiers is in the plant girl. Interesting.' I then threw him out."

"We can now reveal to the others about you two, I feel. It may give you a morale boost, but tell them yourselves that you do not wish to be leader. Okay?"

They paused for a moment, in which time Estre said, *Yes.* "Okay."

We went to the auditorium.

Chapter 20

We summoned all the people of the camp to the auditorium, and waited. We were standing at the stage thing, and discussing on how to reveal it.

"We could just tell them straight forwardly," said Cielo.

"No." I disagreed.

"No. We told you why." That was Pianta.

"We could...have Estre tell them."

They can come out and materialize for three hours, before they must inhabit something. The three of us can do it. It will look dramatic.

I relayed this to them. They agreed. "She says Black." We said at the same time. "She also says the all three of them are pale." That was me.

"Amy says one-oh-one."

"So does Tiers."

Two minutes later, the auditorium was full. "Athorvi." I whispered.

Everyone fell silent, like they just noticed us. We stepped up, and I just summoned some wind, for effect. *Now.*

As if blown out of us, They materialized out of us, Wearing the same black dress, sleeveless, with a bit of flair in it. A bit too dramatic. The wind died down, and everybody was like "What?" and "who?"

"As you all know, I am Der Estre Magier. Ella Elementa is my host. Many of you may have wondered where my peers were. Well…"

She indicated to her sides, to Amy and Tiers. "Amy Elementa and Tiers Elementa."

"We have chosen our hosts."

"I'm going to a stars girl, and Tiers is in a plant girl."

"Cielo Estrella is my host."

"And Pianta Jeune is mine."

They blew themselves back inside us, and there was a stunned silence. Then, the stars and Plant people said unanimously, "We want you as our leader!"

"No, we can't."

"We mustn't."

"Why not?" Someone shouted, almost whining.

"As we need Estre, Amy, and Tiers."

"We need to keep them from being captured, and the only way to do that is…"

"To avoid being captured ourselves. We can't do that as leaders."

I stepped up. "For some reason Malvagita wants leaders-"

Some black mist entered the room. Who else could it be?

I whispered, "Da eis infirma forma." Make them solid and weaken them as well.

The mist solidified, becoming Cattiva and Malvagita, but they were far from weak, which is what I was intending. That is to say, they were normal. I had decided to use the ancient language for all spells, but Estre said, *Don't.* I didn't.

"Oh, don't panic. I'm just here to make a deal." He held out his hand, and Apprendista appeared. She had a black dress on, and black chains around her hands, legs, and neck. "Torquem Albo apud nigrum. Relinquere kyria duces." Tie the White with Black chains. Leave the

86

leader unbound. Every single person in the hall, with the exception of Juliet, was captured. Okay, I was only nearly captured. I said, "Stamatíste tou mágou mágia méchri kai na boreí na!"

It didn't chain me. Wonderful. I turned back, and said, "Da mihi armaturam Lutetiola." Armor shimmered around me. I then said, "Freigabe." The chains clattered down. That was easy.

I turned and started to draw my sword, and saw that Malvagita had a short black knife in his hand, and it was pointed straight at Apprendista's heart.

"Stab me. I would rather die."

"I know. That is why I am not doing it."

They turned their back to me, and I sneaked upon them. Cattiva noticed me, and drew twin knives out of thin air.

"Is that a trend or what? Getting things out of thin air?"

He didn't reply. He struck. I dodged and drew a sword. "Faites le twinella." Duplicate the sword. I got twin swords. Malvagita said, "Nigrescere. Exarmo." Stop. Disarm.

The swords and knives flew out of our hands. He sent a black orb towards me, and I did a kind of back flip. The orb dissolved. I reached the others. "Frítt á þremur." I whispered to them, in Icelandic. I don't know why, it just came to me. *Free on three.*

"Come on, What did you tell them?" Malvagita asked, almost carelessly. "Some new code, I think?"

I tapped the back of my feet thrice. We all yelled, "Friegabe!"

Everybody was freed. The trio disappeared, and reappeared on stage. Apprendista on my side, and the two of them behind and in front of me. Cattiva sent a straight stab, which I ducked, but he slashed with his other knife as soon as I straightened up, leaving a deep cut. I stumbled back, into Malvagita's waiting arms. He had his sword at his ready, and he casually placed it at my neck. "Hey," He whispered. "I never repeat my mistakes. You do. Now, tell them all to shut up."

"Why can't you? Lost your voice box?"

"Cattiva?"

He stepped forward, and make his knife press my burn, and it burned so much, I screamed. I couldn't move, but I could feel blood moving from the infinity, and everybody gasped. Cattiva removed his knife, and I looked at my arm. The Infinity was now a deep cut, rather than a burn.

"Now, about my deal, it's this. Give me Teire willingly, or I'll take Her by force, after killing Elementare here, and wounding Ella. Make your pick."

"A deal has two sides, Ubella," said Juliet with malevolence.

"Ah, yes. Juliet, You and Ella can have apprentices, without me either taking or killing them. But, it can't be a leader."

"How long do we have to take this decision?"

"The rest of the day. I want her before 12 noon tomorrow, or it will be option B. Clear?"

"Crystal. Oh, and one more thing. Is this negotiable?"

"A bit."

"Release other leaders."

"No." The blade was pushed further in.

"Release Apprendista." I was thinking, *Stop already, woman!*

"If you cooperate, yes."

"Okay. Let's go, people."

They all walked out, a few of the Moon people looking back in concern at Apprendista.

Once the auditorium was empty, Malvagita grabbed my arm, and pressed the infinity, and then removed the sword. I doubled up in pain, and after some time, he let it go. Basically, he threw me towards Apprendista, whose chains had been released with that of the masses.

"Reima," Bind. He said that almost lazily. We were tied, Apprendista with her arms behind, and I with my arms forwards.

"I have a feeling that you may try to cause some mischief. So, let's talk. You decided to go to the Library."

"Yes. Who gave you the lenses?"

"Oh, Custos Himself."

"He said you never went there."

"No, Master didn't. I did." Cattiva interrupted.

"So, when was that?"

"On my first trip here."

"What lenses are you guys talking about? What Library?"

"Nothing, Apprendista." I shifted to the ancient language, forcing him to reply in kind.

"I think I know what your experiment is."

"What?"

"You are planning to reduce our strength. Taking away the leaders can do that."

"Interesting theory."

"Am I right?"

He pressed the infinity, and said, "Shut up. Sleep."

The last thing I remember thinking was that Malvagita uses only simple spells in the ancient language, and dark ones too.

Chapter 21

I had a dreamless sleep, for the first night in camp. You would think that it is a good thing, but it is not. I was surrounded by nothing but black. I was relieved when I heard a voice saying, "Hyponisa… Hyponisa." I woke up.

"Curate abscissi." Cure the cut.

The cut was healed, and they tied and gagged us manually, with the same things that they'd used in the Recharge room. They propped us against the wall, and a group of people appeared. They were Juliet, Stren, Pianta, Cielo, and Teire. I slumped my shoulders.

"I give myself up to you, Ubella, but only after you swear that you will not go back on your word."

"Oh, I swear."

I successfully spat out my gag, and shouted, "In the Prima Lingua!"

"Oh, very well. Viot dixi condicionibus testor sectari, dummodo vestrum agis." I swear to follow the conditions, provided that you are doing the same. "Satisfied? And how did you spit that out?"

"Figure it out yourself."

"Okay." He stepped up to me and started that burn to cut thing again, but I said, "Allez." He flew back, and then I said "Freigabe."

The bonds around me released, and I leapt up, but by then, Cattiva had got his knife out and had pushed me to the wall. "Hah. Got you back for the mind thing."

"Really? I thing I owe you a few stabs now. That is-"

"I know what you mean."

Malvagita got up again, and went to Teire. He grabbed her hand, and the three of them, and the black chains dissolved into black mist. Big surprise.

Estre?

Yeah?

Why were you silent?

The darkness.

Oh.

I go to Apprendista, and helped her to Juliet.

"How are you, App?" She asked, with nothing masking the concern in her voice.

"Another Elementa? You'd think that there were an unlimited set of them, kept for the wars, right?"

"Good, you're fine."

"How on earth did you guess?"

They cracked a smile, and I did the intros. "Stren – Apprendista. Apprendista – Stren."

"What's an Elementare?"

"It's a person who has got the other powers by practice." Apprendista said. "You Elementas have got it easy. I keep telling Juliet that."

"Oh."

During this nice little conversation, I scanned App's mind. It was clean. No black. No balance. That way, we can actually say that there is a balance. I'll try not to bore you with math.

"Let's check all vitals, shall we?"

"I'm fine Ella. Look."

She Jumped up, and down, and did a bit of gymnastics. "Tadaa!"

We left, trying not to look too happy. App has a way of livening things up. Apparently, the others thought so too, as they were all like, "Hey, App!"

We went to the Elementa room, and I invited them in. "Come in, Pianta, Cielo, Apprendista. Next time needs another invite."

Stren raised an eyebrow, and as soon as we were in, he said, "Explain. You promised."

"Good memory."

"Get on with it."

I raised an eyebrow at Juliet, and she nodded. Estre said yes too. So I launched into the story, missing the parts that Juliet must not know, and those that the others must not know.

"A lot has happened since I left."

"Yup."

"Is that all?"

"Yes."

I lied, obviously.

"Say it in Prima Lingua."

"Do you know it?"

"I overheard Mauvaise and Ubella practice."

"Quod est in omnibus." I couldn't have lied, so I thought, *That I can tell you now.*

"What is Prima Lingua?" Stren asked.

"The oldest Language of Magic." I replied.

Estre, now as powerful a six magicians, partly came out and said, "The oldest of all the languages. Greek and Latin are the next."

"What about Egyptian?"

"Another Place. Independent Language." Said Apprendista.

"So, What's the plan?"

"The plan is to – Wait." I muttered and Anti dark spell, and Estre did one in the ancient language. "The plan is to get the leaders-"

"To swear an oath in the ancient language-"

"Thereby preventing them-"

"From lying."

"Are you two able to read each other's minds or something?"

"No, we're two in one and one," said Estre.

"What!?!" Yelled Juliet, Stren, and Apprendista at the same time.

"Two minds, a main body, and a body that can exist only temporarily."

"Juliet!" I yelled.

"What?"

"Let's get an apprentice."

"Okay. Who are you taking?"

I did a quick mental conversation with Estre. *Stren?* I asked.

Ok.

"Elementa, serez-vous mon apprenti?"

Stren paused, and said, "Sì."

"La couleur est noire."

When can we do this?

Tomorrow.

"When can we do this?" asked Juliet.

"Tomorrow. Who are you taking?"

"Juliet? I don't think I can." said Apprendista.

"Why not, App?"

"I'm tainted."

I disagreed, but I kept it to myself.

"I think I'll take Selena Soliel."

"Who is she?" I asked.

"Most powerful Sun Girl."

"Not a good Idea. Take a moon girl." Said Estre.

"Why?"

"That is your best bet. Take her while she still has a leader."

"Lau Mond."

"Most powerful moon girl?"

"Aye. Those two are the third and fourth most powerful Magicians that are, or were when I was here, in Camp."

"Where does Arbre stand?"

"Fifth, Last I checked, but probably seventh now."

"Seventh?"

"Depending on where you and Stren are placed."

"Let's go call Lau?"

"Yes. C'mon."

On that happy note (no sarcasm), we left the Elementa room.

Chapter 22

Juliet chose her colour as blue, the Nahunta (Perfect) colour, she felt. We did our things without any Disruptions, and got to know each other. I taught Stren what I had learnt from my various sources, keeping some information to myself, of course.

We decided to rank the Elementals. Juliet graded the Subs. We went to the rooms one by one, obviously. I went in, and the room was, for once, with the perfect ratio of white to black.

"Hello, Ella Elementa. Step into the circle."

I stepped into the circle, and looked at Juliet. "Hold out your hand." I did that. A little obstacle course sort of thing appeared, and she said, "You will be timed. Several rounds will determine the most powerful Elemental. This is one where you know what to expect. All your magic will be tested, starting from the least powerful, and going to the most powerful. In general. Your time starts...now!"

The circle disappeared, and so did the obstacle course. I said, "Riveli voi stessi." The course reappeared. I was in the middle of it. I whispered the rarest of the invisibility spells, "See me you shall not, though I be in front of you. Hear me you shall not, though I say much to you. This I say to my enemy, to those who wish to harm me, and to those who wish to test my abilities, except The lead one." Very detailed, but it works even when I say it in English, which I did. I became invisible. None could hear me. But I still had to be careful enough to let none feel me.

I heard Estre involuntarily tense. I checked my amulet, and it was full. I saw…a flower maze. I just crushed them. They regrew. I burnt them. They regrew. I flew over them. They grew. I stopped them until I crossed, and ran. I met a plant guy. I decapitated him with my sword and kept moving. Then rainbow. Then Gems. Animals. Stars. Sun. Moon. I Met Fiore. He was there as an Earth guy. I trumped his earth powers, and knocked him out. Then came Lau as an air girl. She had earned her amulet already, so it was not as easy as Fiore, but I did it. I met Stren. He was a water guy. He said, "Your objective is to retrieve a note from the lead Elementa from the Fire person who will fight you."

"How do I know you are not lying?"

"You don't."

He attacked, and I combined the powers of the three other Elements and sent him out of the course.

CRAAACK!

There was Juliet, standing with her arms flaming. Fire. Duh.

"Look into my eyes, Oh powerful Elementa. Tell me what you see."

"I don't even need to look for that. Your eyes are glowing. You are attempting a *hypnotizovat*, a Mesmer. How obvious. It would be easier to do this." I raised my arm, and said, "Vos gré est la mienne."

Her eyes immediately became normal, then white through and through, and she said, "My Will is yours. Tell me what it is that I need to do."

I first raised shields around myself, and said, "Take that bit of metal there." I pointed to a patch of lutetium. "Make it a cage, and charm it such that whoever enters it will lose their power unless faced with predominantly dark forces."

"As you will, Oh Great One."

She did it as willingly as anything, and said, "It is done."

"Enter it and lock yourself in it, and say Je jure de répondre à toutes vos questiols en toute honnêteté. Say it with will."

I made her swear in the ancient language to tell me the truth.

She went in and locked herself. Then I remembered that an oath in the ancient language works only if the swearer does it of his or her own freewill. So, I told her, "Never mind the saying part. Tell me a spell that will strengthen the metal. Make a hoop that can be put on top of the cage. Fast."

She did that in seconds. I attached the hoop to the top of the cage, and told the spell. I then said, "Tie yourself with that and tell me all the weak spots in that."

"There are none, oh powerful Elementa."

I removed the Mesmer. Her eyes became normal, and she closed her eyes for a second. I made the bonds tighter.

"Let me go, Ella. What if Malvagita attacks now?"

"Then the cage will disappear, and I can untie you."

She tried to struggle, but I had Bonded the metal with my fist. I took energy from a tree and tightened the bonds. She squeaked in pain. I told her, "Answer me. Do you have any note from the lead Elementa?"

"Yes."

"Give it."

She put her fingertips in her pocket, and I felt her trying to do Magic. I squeezed the bonds and she yelled. No, screamed.

"Loosen them!"

"Where is the note, Juliet?"

"Up my sleeve!"

I magically lifted a twig, and keeping my fist closed, brought out the note. It said, '*Your next task is to locate and fight the four most powerful magicians of camp (according to the last count, not the one going on now) one by one. You must do it in 25 minutes or less to get to the top position.'*

"Who are the four most powerful magicians?"

"I can't tell! Loosen the bonds!"

I tightened them, and said, "First tell me according to the previous calculations."

"Pianta! Cielo! Selena! Lau!"

I loosened them and whispered a spell. It translates into, "Make the cage invisible. Make the person inside it invisible. Do not let anybody see, hear, or touch any part of her or the cage. Go high up. Make the bonds around her tight enough to prevent her movement, but not tighter. I must be able to see her."

As simple as that. I went in search of Lau.

Chapter 23

I didn't find her where I left her, so I charged my amulet (With chargers I had created myself), reinforced my energy and shields, and whispered a Find. I found all of them.

"Oh, there's something that the note forgot to mention."

"Yes, and it is crucial."

"We do often travel in packs."

"And you must battle us together if you must."

They surrounded me and started circling. I whispered a spell in the ancient language. Translation, "Make sure none can suppress my power, not even my own inventions." No sooner than I said that, did all four of them say, "Vos gré est la mienne!"

I lost control of my body, and said like I had nothing else as important to say, "My will belongs to the four of you. Do what you want with it."

"Tie yourself to that tree," said Pianta.

"As tightly as you can." Added Cielo.

I dutifully did that, but there were seconds when I did have control. I waited for that second later, but it didn't come right then.

"Do you feel a rope there?" That was Selena.

"Yes, oh powerful Sun."

"Pull it, and lean your head backwards."

I had tied myself like I was hugging the tree, and a few bits of each of their powers came falling down. They merged into the ropes that I had used, and I felt a link to their hands.

"Put your head against the bark of the tree."

"Tell us what you feel."

"A button."

"Press it."

I did that, and my neck was held fast to the tree. I felt a spasm of control, and I tried to untie myself, but my muscles didn't obey. I realized that this was to keep the body from numbing or something of the sort.

"Scream if it hurts."

One of them squeezed the bonds. Then two. Then three. Then four. Then they made them tighter. I think they connected it to both their hands. I screamed.

They removed the Mesmer. I immediately untied myself and yelled, "Freigabe! Stupéfiez! Rendez sans connaissance! Betäuben Sie! Stordisca!"

The four of them fell to the ground. There were notes tied to their wrists. I magically removed them and read them. It made no sense. I put them one on top of another, and it made sense. It said, *Congratulations. You did it in five minutes. Your task is to get out of this course and go to the Auditorium. There, you will have to fight with the ten magicians below you in the power line. You have 10 minutes to accomplish this.*

I did a Find for Stren, and got out of the course. I flew to the auditorium, and readied myself for the fight. I landed through the roof. I realized that my invisibility spell had worn of. I started to do it again, but about four people grabbed me from the back and shut my mouth. I thought, *Stupéfiez les personnes qui me touchent!* Stun the people who are touching me. They collapsed. The other 6 were invisible. "Riveli voi stessi." They shimmered into existence. I grabbed my sword, and said, "Enlevez leur magie à moins que quelque chose les attaques principalement foncées." They tried a spell and it didn't work. I said, "Bloccaggio," while sending some fire-water balls to them. Done. White mist curled off Stren's sword (Top ten! I am *so* proud.), and it became a microphone (Really, Juliet?) "Go to the Auditorium, Ella."

I went to the Auditorium.

Chapter 24

I thought we had been sent there to find our position on the list. I was only partially right.

"We have a draw for the first place-"

"What!" shouted 162 voices.

"Between?" Yelled Pianta.

"First, I'll tell you how many we have. There's one for the first, third, and fifth places."

"Oh my God. That is *rare*." I whispered to Pianta.

"Really?" She said, sarcastically.

"We'll start from fifth place. Selena Soliel and Lau Mond."

They stepped forward. "You know the drill. Winner of the duel is the winner of the place. Begin."

Immediately, Selena sent a sun at Lau, which got countered with a moon. Lau Retaliated with a fire and water combo (My type), and Selena sent another earth and water one. Then – well, you get the Idea. Suddenly, they both ran out of magic, amulet wise and otherwise. Selena was the first to react. She drew her sword, and had a triumphant smile on her face. But Lau dodged and knocked the sword out of Selena's hands and gave a triumphant yell.

"You were always over-confident, sis."

"You always say that!"

"That always happens!"

Before further argument could break out, Juliet said, "Fifth place – Lau. Sixth place – Selena. Go recharge."

They left, arguing as only sisters could.

"The next draw is between Pianta and Cielo. Yes, Again."

"They always duel each other."

Their duel went on pretty much the same way as the previous one, except here, Pianta won. Apart from that…

"Third place, Pianta. Fourth place – Cielo."

They went to recharge.

"The draw for the first place, between the two most powerful magicians not including the leaders and the Darks, is between Ella Elementa and Stren Elementa!"

We stepped forward, and struck each other with a mix of two different types of magic. We did all 132 combinations. Then we did two at a time, three at a time, and four at a time. I decided to go big and do something unexpected. I gathered my energy and sent a copy of my amulet with blackened vines as the separators, and an E (For Elementa, by the way) in the center (in fire). It was meant to capture, unless he did the same thing. It was very powerful. Stren did the same thing at the same time, and they glided towards each other slowly, while we collapsed. They hovered near the stage, fighting their own battle there for a few seconds. There was no more energy in my amulet, so I got up and drew my sword. So did Stren. We both Dueled for a while, and out swords broke. We used daggers, knives, and Spears, nothing worked. We had to go hand to hand, when I went to his mind and I tried, but I had already taught him that. We did a thing with both, stretching our resources to the limit. We finally collapsed after some more time, to a stunned silence.

"There is another draw for First place! We cannot do anything else about it. Well done, both of you. Maybe later, but only after the war. So, the list. Ella cum Stren, Pianta, Cielo, Selena, Lau, Stervia, Kleur…"

I heard my position, and grabbed Stren's hand, who did the same. We left to recharge and Refresh.

———⊰≋⊱———

Over the course of the next few days, I had a hectic schedule. The 'All Elements' thing that we summoned were still there, and it was quiet an attraction. It took no energy from us that I could feel.

While I was walking around, I came across a red stone.

That is a communication stone, Said Estre. *The rest of them are lost.*

Does it contain any spells?

No.

I went to Stren, and got him to Draw seven of them, two blue, two green, and two yellow. I gave him and Pianta a green one each, Cielo and Lau a blue each, and Selena a yellow. I gave the seventh to Stervia, a stones girl. Most powerful. Again. We were "The Seven", most powerful, blah blah blah. We decided to practice our magic together, and stay together, and all that. It all went on smoothly, until the next incident.

It was the end of Stren's shift, and I went there a little early. The other five of the Seven were there too. Suddenly, there was a clap of thunder and two flashes of lightning. The lightning hit two trees, and from the ashes rose – *gasp!* – Malvagita and Cattiva. They flew forward, and tried to shoot through between Selena and Pianta. They stopped them, obviously, but the Anima Tueur appeared and battled them. Five others ran to help. I sent Kleur to Juliet for help. Stren and I then flew to Malvagita and Cattiva. A fierce double duel sort of thing followed. Neither side got and advantage. Then Juliet arrived, and Malvagita flashed a triumphant smile. He sent a blast of Dark magic strait at my chest, and I was hurled back. By the sound of It, Cattiva did the same to Stren. I was about to get up when I felt a cold feeling above my heart. I looked up and saw the Anima Tueur towering above me. It began to lean down to reach for my soul, when Malvagita yelled, "Stop!"

The Anima Tueur turned to the next target, Stren, but I grabbed a spear that Stren had drawn. I drew my arm back, and stabbed the Anima Tueur successively in two places, the head and the heart. At the same time, Stren cut of its head. Ew. It gave a wail and dissipated into Black mist, wherein white mist emerged and enveloped the creature, sending it to its doom.(Bit dramatic, right?)

While all these dramatic things were happening, Juliet was dueling both Cattiva and Malvagita at the same time. Cattiva seemed ready to collapse, but Malvagita seemed to be doing things rather effortlessly. I went there, and Malvagita said, "Good job. I didn't think you'd know that bit of information. Now, look." He said a command in Prima Lingua, and Everybody Except Malvagita, Cattiva, and Juliet were bound from head to foot. He smiled at me, and I understood. Juliet was next.

Another flash of lightning, and the three of them disappeared. We were untied, and I started a Find. However, Estre said, panicking, *Don't.*

I didn't.

At that moment, I realized something. With Juliet gone, authority was automatically transferred to the next Elementa in line. That meant I was the leader. I Sent Stren back and did my shift.

The War had begun, and I was the Leader.

Part 2

Chapter 1

Hey, my name is Stren Elementa. When you're done reading this, you'll probably find out the reason as to why several things happened in the world in the summer. I found out that I was a magician a few months ago, and I, quite frankly, wish I hadn't. If I hadn't, then I would not have gotten stuck in the middle of a war, and wouldn't have nearly gotten killed as a result of it.

Soon after I found out I was a magician (or Elemental, whatever), I found this camp, and got knee deep in that war I was talking about. A few weeks later, two evil dudes, Malvagita Ubella and Cattiva Mauvaise, captured our leader, Juliet Elementa. And no, she is not my sister.

So, I became second in command, with another girl called Ella Elementa (She isn't my sister either, thank God) as the Leader. We had to break the news to the people who didn't know it, and so we called a meeting at the auditorium.

"So, You're all probably wondering why we called you all here. Well, there has been another capture." I should explain. Those two evil dudes were capturing the leaders of the 12 types of magic.

"Who, Ella?" Asked a girl. *Luna,* I remembered.

She took a deep breath. "Juliet." She said bluntly.

The camp erupted into utter chaos. *Ella can't control them*, I realized. A lady suddenly appeared next to Ella and yelled, "Everybody, SHUT UP!" That was Estre, or Der Estre Magier. Ella Hosts her. Actually, she is officially dead. Weird? Welcome to my world.

"Listen," she continued. "We cannot change what happened. What we can do is train and make sure we do not let the leaders down. We need to be strong enough to defeat them. Malvagita and Cattiva probably want us to lose heart. We cannot let that happen. We need to be strong. Listen to Ella. Right now, we need to plan your training schedule. We will be ready." She went back into Ella.

Pianta and Cielo, who host Estre's friends, came and stood on either side of us (Ella and me). Ella summoned a board sort of thing, and sent the Elementals' symbols that Ella and I had summoned to the side. She said, "Okay, people. We need to do something about the defense situation. We'll make the shifts shorter. So that's 160 campers, 40 per shift, four shifts. If we make it 8 shifts, no camper will need to stay at the defenses for more than 2 hours. The Elementa's shifts will be for three hours at a stretch."

I continued when she paused. "We also need to increase our magical abilities to include other Elements. So, Ella, Selena, Lau, Pianta, Cielo, Stervia and I will teach the rest of you how to control the other Elements."

This continued for a while, and we all got our scheduled settled. I was to teach the Sun and the Moon cabins. I expected that it would be tough as their powers were both similar and different. So they'd probably argue a lot. Well, every job had its ups and downs. I just had to find the ups. Joy.

Ella was spending most of her time in a library, which she had found with Pianta. Apparently, the library was called the Great Library, and every single camper had visited it once. Well, truth be told, I was not keen to do that at all.

Anyhow, one day, Ella called us to the library. I couldn't go, so I listened to their conversation with my mind. She showed us a scroll. *Wonderful. Can I go now?* I asked her. Then Cielo said, "Oh. My. God. Where did you find it? It is the ultimate secret to keep the Dark out! That is so AWESOME!"

"What!?!" Screamed Pianta and Stervia.

How can that- I spotted a black shape flying towards us. It was those two, Malvagita and Cattiva. *Red alert. It's those two again. Backup?*

I'm on my way, Stren. I heard the answering thought from Ella. I hoped she'd hurry up. The last time he came, I nearly had my soul sucked out of my body. I was *not* keen for a replay.

Malvagita was almost across, and Cattiva was not that far behind. I drew (Literally) myself a bow and quiver full of arrows (One of my useful talents), and started shooting them. I got Malvagita between the shoulder blades, and he stumbled. I tied him up in vines, and started saying the word for capture. "Blocc-"

I was interrupted by Cattiva, who came at me with a black knife. So, I was engaged in a fight with two evil dudes, which I could not possibly hope to win. Fortunately for me, Ella arrived and engaged Malvagita in a duel. By that time, we had gotten the undivided attention of the entire shift, and some others also came and stood aside. Unfortunately, some of them were the leaders. I heard Malvagita say something to Ella, who paled. Cattiva sent a bolt of Black energy to capture me. He didn't say the word for capture, however. Malvagita did the same to Ella. She seemed to recover from her shock, and sent white tendrils of energy to break the cage. I did the same thing. We managed to break the cage, but by then, Malvagita had already sent four bolts out from his hand to the leaders. We sent white bolts to counter them, but it was too late. The leaders disappeared, along with the evil dudes.

I walked up to Ella. "Another meeting?"

She scowled. "Yeah."

I sighed. Time to get bored.

Chapter 2

"Who knew a set of 12 people had so many questions?" I asked as we were walking out of the Auditorium.

"You're a fine one to talk." She replied. "You had more questions on your first day here than what the whole lot of them put to us now."

"Did not!" I felt the blood rush to my cheeks. We argued like this while we walked to the Elemental house.

She went to her shift. I, in the mean time, did my bit of training. Estre agreed to train me while Ella was on her shift. We practiced single summons of the Elements, merges of two, three, and four. Then we went to the charging area, and I charged my amulet. Then, I went to the shift and relieved Ella.

Nothing happened during my shift. I guess they were taking a time out while they did their 'experiment'. By 'they' I mean Malvagita and Cattiva. Ella sent Kleur, a stars girl, to take my place, and I went to Ella.

"What is it?" I asked her.

"This will work. That's why he got the other leaders so soon."

"What will work?"

She showed me the same scroll. I took it, this time, and opened it. I did a quick read. "Wow." I said, utterly shocked. The scroll was a full and full shield against the Dark side. They couldn't enter Camp in any way except by walking (or running) in, they couldn't See us (With a capital 'S'), and so on, and so forth. "When can we start?"

She smiled. "As soon as the others get here."

We waited, and I grew impatient. I sent a mind message through the communication stones that Ella made me draw. *Where are you guys!?!*

No need to shout, Stren. We're training. It will take some time for us to come. Stervia replied.

"They're training. It'll take them ages to get here." I whined.

She grinned and said, "That's 'cause they don't look for the first reason to leave training, unlike a certain someone out here."

I scowled. "Well, I know a way to get them out."

"Never mind that." She said. "How were we able to produce the White mist? I've never been able to do that before."

"What!" I yelled. "But-but you did it like you've done it before. You were so fast!"

Estre simmered into existence next to me. "I do not know how you did it. However, I know that it will be easier for you to do it again. You are more powerful. I think you guys will… Never mind. The important thing is that you will now be able to do magic better and easier."

That was good. But I wondered what she was about to say. Ella tried the mist again, and it came. I added my own to it, and It glowed really bright. It rose and went high above camp. Then, It spread over camp like a blanket. Black mist came towards it as well, and Ella started to send some white mist at it, but stopped. Estre probably asked her to stop. The black mist joined the blanket of white mist as well, and the entire thing disappeared. Estre came out and yelled, "Okay, all of you. Come to the auditorium. Yes, even those of you in the shift."

We all went to the auditorium, and had another meeting.

———◆———

That night, I had a dream. And it was not just any dream either. It seemed so real, I was sure it was happening, or going to happen, or had happened before.

Malvagita and Cattiva were in the house of the Elementas, and were chatting about Ella, and the challenge she posed. I came in closer and heard them. I could not see them, so I didn't know who said what.

"We need to get rid of that girl."

"Well, duh. But the question is, how?"

"We just need to-"

"No. We need to get rid of that boy as well. We cannot just go there and get rid of them; we have to plan it. They are *powerful.* More than you are, in fact."

"But-"

"No buts, little apprentice. Let's check on the 'leaders', shall we?"

The dream blurred and ended. After that, it was just white.

———◆———

I woke up to the shrill beeps of my alarm clock. I dragged myself out of bed, washed, dressed, and ran to the walls. Ella was at the center, waiting.

"You're late." She said as I ran up.

"Sorry. I came as fast as I could." I said.

"Sorry doesn't cut it. You've got to get up earlier. Split your sleep hours. Got it?"

"Yes, ma'am!" I saluted. She smiled and shook her head.

"Well?" She asked. "Are you going to get up here or what?"

"Sorry, again." I scrambled up the lutetium wall. They had magical footholds, of course, so only a predominantly white person could get up. She just rolled her eyes and jumped off.

"You could have just used Magic." She admonished. Then she did a find and disappeared to the auditorium, presumably. And then I got bored out of my life for the next three hours.

I decided to go to the auditorium after my shift, when I heard a blood-curling scream. Then another. And another. I ran towards the sound of the first one, and found Ella at the center of the defense system. She was on her back, her eyes open, but staring away, like she was looking at something at a distance. I touched her forehead, and sent my mind into hers. I felt two other minds, Pianta's and Cielo's. I felt a white-hot burning somewhere, but I couldn't place it. I withdrew my mind and looked at her hand. There was a burn on her arm, an 'Infinity', and it was glowing. I frowned. I decided to try to heal it.

"Sanare!" Heal! Instead of healing, It glowed even brighter, and burned me. I looked at my arm, and saw a burn growing, and realized that I had to end the spell. I did that, but It kept expanding. There were twelve spiraling lines running up my arm, and I was losing Energy rapidly. Ella got up, and I fell, blacking out.

Chapter 3

The next time I woke up, I was in the infirmary. I glanced at my arm, but all that was there was a burn that looked like a bracelet. I got up, and asked the attending Elemental, "Can I get out of here?"

She turned towards me and said, "Nope." It was Selena. "Ella's orders."

"C'mon! Please?"

"No, Stren."

"How long have I been here?"

"Long enough, I feel. But Ella said that she needs to check on something."

I grunted. Why did she need to keep me here? Ella entered. Pianta and Cielo closely followed her. "We need to go to the House of the Elementas." She said. She grabbed my hand, and we 'teleported' to the house of the Elementas.

"How did you get the burn to become so small?" I asked.

She smiled grimly. "I use my mist. Show me your arm." I did that and she said, "There is a way to get rid of this completely."

"Great!" Yelled Pianta and Cielo.

"Not so. On the contrary, it is terrible."

I frowned. "How so?"

"We need both the Pure Forms."

"Excuse me!?!" The rest of us yelled. I know, it was a lot of yelling.

She sighed. "We need both Black and White mist. The 'mist' is the Pure form of the magic."

It took a second for me to realize what she had just said. "You mean... We need to Summon the Black Mist."

"Or endure the burns."

So we were stuck between a rock and a hard place. "Well," I started. Pianta interrupted.

"We can summon the mist just this once."

"NO!!!" Yelled Ella. "Don't you see? That's why he gave us the burns. He wants us to make that choice! He wants us to turn our amulets Black."

I decided that it was ripe time to continue what I was saying. "We'll not summon black mist, we'll cover the burn with White mist, and try to neutralize the effects of the burn as much as we can."

"That's all very well for you, but we can't do that yet." Said Cielo

Ella sent some White Mist towards Pianta and Cielo. It wrapped them up, but not for long. It expanded, and finally burst. It was clear that they both had summoned the Mist. "You were saying?" Ella asked, while reabsorbing her Mist. I suppressed a smile. She had a way of making people go speechless, and that's what she did now. Of course, she usually used Magic, but that's a different issue.

"Well?" She asked. "Stren, Pianta, go to your shift. Cielo, let's train." She ran off, and Cielo followed her. Pianta gave a disgusted sound, and we went to our shift, where I sat in boredom for another two hours.

⊷⊰⊱⊶

I went to the auditorium to train, and defeated everybody there in duels. Then it became two against one, three against one, four against one...

In the last combination of four against one, I felt a pressure building up outside my mind. I realized that whoever it was, he was Dark and Powerful. I strengthened my defenses, and got ready for a fight. In the meantime, I indicated to the people I was training against to stop Fighting. I closed my eyes and braced for impact. It came about 5 seconds later. Dark mist hurtled towards my mind, and I resisted. I managed to push the Darkness off for a few minutes, and so it Solidified. Malvagita. The one and only. He tried to walk straight through the mist, but he banged into a Shark. Cool, huh?

He growled and drew a sword. I recalled what Ella said about her first MindFight with the guy. *He can't use Magic.* Well, I definitely could. I became human and drew my Sword. I also summoned a mist sword and a mist sheath that looked so real that he could not figure out which was which.

He grinned and said, "Wasting your Energy."

"Yeah, Ubella?" I tried to throw him out of my Mind. "Fuera!"

He raised his sword and threw it at my heart. I couldn't stop it, so I tried to dodge it. It would have hit me, but an arm entered my field of vision, and hit it out of the way. It was Ella. She was wearing lutetium Armor, which was why it didn't cut her. She already had some cuts, however, but that didn't stop her.

"Stren!" She yelled. "Permission!"

I whispered, "I give Ella Elementa permission to use magic in my mind during this attack." Then I yelled out loud, "Done!"

She defended me, and Cattiva entered in the mean time. I made him fight me, instead of going to his 'master's' aid. Over his shoulder, I saw Ella get subdued, and Pianta and Cielo appearing. They subdued

Malvagita. I, however, allowed myself to get distracted, and Cattiva gave me a cut on my shoulder. I cursed and tried to stab him, but he disappeared. Then I raised the defenses around my mind. Ella noticed the cut, and got out. I got opened my eyes, and saw Ella tending to… My shoulder? I looked, but her hair blocked my view.

"How bad is it?" I croaked.

She looked at me with unshielded concern. "Bad. Why didn't you use Prima Lingua?"

Prima Lingua was an ancient language that Ella had learnt a few days before Juliet got captured.

"I forgot, I guess."

She blew. "You *forgot*!?! How can you forget the very thing that got him out of my mind the first time and the countless other times he came in?"

I looked down sheepishly. "Sorry."

That didn't help. "And on top of that, you gave the permission in English. That is useless unless I hear you." She paused. "On a brighter note, Lau has just finished her other Elements training, so we have three 'All Elements' Elementals to do this stuff. Of course, that means I will train you in my spare time." I groaned, and she glared at me. "You definitely need it. We'll focus more on MindFights. And this time, I'm not going to hold back."

"Yes, Ella." I said. I tried a salute, but my shoulder ruined it.

Her lips drew into a thin line. "Apprendista?" She called.

"Yeah, Ella?"

"Take over Stren's shift for the time being, will you?"

"Sure." Ella pulled me up, and we went to the house of the Elementas.

Chapter 4

Well, the first thing that we did was, obviously, practicing MindFights. We finished with that as well. In fact, I think that's what we were doing the whole time.

So, here's how it went.

I retreated into my mind, and put up every defense I could think of. I nodded, and immediately, Ella broke them. Talk about demoralization. I tried to brace myself, and waited for impact, but it never came. I relaxed a bit, and vaguely heard Ella yell at me. I opened my eyes, and Ella was *angry*.

"You idiot, you forgot to put the main defense, the 'anti-magician thingy', as you called it. Stren, concentrate! You can't afford to forget things like this in an actual fight! Now, get ready again, and do it properly this time."

I did it properly the next time, and fended her off. Then, she solidified partially (we were both in the 'mist' forms at that time), and walked right through me. Then she became mist again (What's the word for that? Vaporized? Mistified?), and surrounded me. Of course, part of her mind just did some stuff with the rest of the mind-me, and in seconds, I was vanquished. *How?* I thought. *How was she able to defeat me so easily, when it was a draw during evaluation?*

Because, she replied. I winced. I forgot that she could hear my thoughts now. *I pay attention when Estre teaches me. You need to start doing that.* She withdrew from my mind, and I opened my eyes.

"I'm gonna go train the other Elementals. Coming?" She asked.

"Sure."

We walked to the auditorium. By the time we got there, two Elements were already there, Plant and Flower. They were, of course, arguing, as one might expect exact opposites to argue.

"Ruhe," said Ella, tiredly. I tried to speak, but I couldn't. "Sorry," she grinned at me. "Sie können sprechen." She turned to the rest of them. "Now, as I keep reminding you, you are here to train, and in case of my absence or lateness, you must practice. Sie können sprechen. Is that what you call practice?"

"No, Ella." They murmured. "We won't do it again."

"Divide into pairs, no like magic in one group."

They divided, and a guy called Fiore was left. He came to Ella, who sent me to be his partner. Sheesh. He was so going down.

"Plant Elementals, Summon a flower. Yes, You're going to summon the opposite power." They did that, and Ella sent a MindMessage. *That includes you,* she said.

Right, I replied.

I Summoned a flower, but I used my amulet. I turned to Ella, and she was glaring at me. *Do not use the Amulet. That's what you're supposed to do.*

I did that easily, but by the time I finished, Fiore was doing his part (Summoning a vine).

Ella continued with the lesson. "Flower Elementas, make the vine grow. This time, Plant Elementals, make it tough for them."

I grinned and stopped the vine from growing with my amulet. Fiore looked at me and grinned. He closed his eyes, concentrated, and boom! The vine grew.

"Okay," Ella said. Now vice versa."

It went on like this for some time. I got bored, of course, but fortunately, Ella had to go to her shift soon.

———◆———

That night, we had a war game. Lau was doing the guard duty, and Apprendista was to take over after that.

This game, apparently, was a continuation of the previous game and I was supposed to be on the blue team. The teams were as follows:

Red	Blue
Plant	Animal
Stars	Flower
Sun	Moon
Rainbow	Precious stones
Fire	Water
Earth	Air
Ella	**Stren**

My job was to find and capture Ella. For that, I got a team of twelve people (Including me).

We went to the other side and found Ella almost immediately, or rather, she found us. I did an invisibility spell, but the others weren't so lucky. She just threw 11 beads at them and captured them. Then, she whispered something and made them disappear. I sneaked in behind her and yelled, "Ruhe! Bloccaggio!" I managed to capture Ella. Then I took her to the place where we kept the prisoners.

"Good," said Stervia. "You got her. But... where are the rest of them?

"Captured." I replied.

She scowled. "I thought I told you to capture without getting captured."

"I did exactly what you told me to do."

"Don't get technical with me, Stren."

Suddenly, Ella broke down my MindBarriers, and took control over me. She saw all about the defenses that we had put up tonight. Then, Lau made me guard Ella. Immediately after Lau left, Ella did some weird stuff with the earth, and started tapping whatever it was that she made. *Morse code!* I realized. She was getting a message to the others in the group. I tried to get out of her control, but she only tightened her grip.

After some time, Pianta and Cielo came in and 'freed' Ella. I got out of Ella's grip, and teleported away before she could start a single spell. I got behind Lau, and we started infiltrating their stronghold.

Ella, Pianta and Cielo appeared, and sent a combination of 4 Elements each. Ella shouted, "Merger!" The three balls merged, and captured us all. The game was over, and the red team had won.

Chapter 5

Ella woke me up at 4 AM and sent me to my shift. Nothing happened, of course, and I finished my shift at 8 AM. I went and trained with Estre and Lau. Then Lau went to her shift, and Ella came the training arena.

"Are you sure, Estre?" She asked, completely ignoring me.

"Yes. One hundred percent." Estre replied. Then she went into Ella.

"Hey, Ella. 'Sup?" I asked.

"C'mon. We've got work to do." She pulled me to a little room/house thingy that had a mirror on the wall. She put her amulet on the mirror, and disappeared.

Well, said Estre, now in my head. *Put your amulet on the mirror.*

I did that, and found myself in a library.

"Ella!" I yelled. "Another Library?"

"HELLO, ELLA ELEMENTA. WHO'S THIS?" Someone asked.

"That is Stren Elementa, Custos."

"STREN, DID YOU SAY?"

"Yes. Estre believed-"

"ESTRE?"

"Sorry. Elena believed that he might be the one."

"Uh... Ella?" I called. "What's going on?"

I felt a mind scanning my own, and I tried to block it. *Relax, Stren Elementa.* That voice... I had heard it before. I tried to remember where, and a Memory flashed in front of me.

It was about 9 years ago, when I was 6 years old. I was playing with my mum and dad. "Come on, Stren. Get the Frisbee." My mum said. I jumped and got it, and did a little victory dance. Dad ruffled my black hair and gave me a high five. Suddenly, the sky darkened.

"C'mon in, kiddo. Looks like there's gonna be a storm." My dad said.

I pouted. "Just a little longer?" I pleaded. "Please?"

"I don't think it'll do any harm," said mum. "Let's play for some more time." Then, I heard the voice.

"COME TO ME, LITTLE ONE. FREE ME FROM THIS PLACE. COME TO ME, STREN ELEMENTA."

The Memory ended, and I fell to the floor, gasping. "You- You were the one!"

"YES."

"What do you want me for?"

"WILL YOU HOST ME?"

I was shocked. "H-host you?" I stammered.

"YES."

I noticed Estre come out of Ella. She looked at me, and I saw something in her eyes...Happiness? Pride? I couldn't place the Emotion. I took a deep breath. "Yes. I will host you, Ancient one."

Some wind rippled, and a flood of knowledge hit me. I staggered, and then relaxed.

I am In you, Stren Elementa. I was Custos Cartis, Keeper of the scrolls. But now, I am Pas Oloi Elementa, the Second magician.

I noticed that I had closed my eyes once again, and opened them. Ella was leaning over me with a concerned expression on her face.

"Hey! Can we get out of the library now?" Her expression became relieved, and then annoyed.

"Fine. Let's go tell everybody that you're hosting Custos Cartis, otherwise called Pas Oloi Elementa!"

I rolled my eyes and got out.

Chapter 6

"All campers, get to the Practice Arena immediately. That includes those on the Shift." Ella announced.

Everybody came in less than thirty seconds.

Ella stepped forward. "A lot of you may have heard of Pas Olio Elementa, right?"

"No!" Said everybody.

"Okay, long story short, Pas was wounded badly in the Prima Battaglia, the first battle. Elena Elementa tried to save him, but failed. However, Pas's spirit was cursed to guard the knowledge of the ancients, until one day, another Elementa came and freed him from this curse. It was not to be easy, as most of the Elementas did not know of the knowledge, which he guarded under the name of Custos Cartis. However, now, Pas Oloi Elementa's spirit has been freed." There were gasps through the crowd. "Stren Elementa is hosting Pas Oloi Elementa!" She shouted, and the Elementals Cheered.

She knows how to use things to her advantage, said Pas admiringly.

Yeah. I said absently. I was thinking about whether Malvagita and Cattiva could actually see this, or See this, whatever is the case.

Ella interrupted my thoughts and said, "Let's go, Stren."

"Where?" I asked.

She rolled her eyes. "To train, duh. Let's see whether your powers have increased."

I groaned. Pas, on the other hand, seemed very enthusiastic. *Come on, boy. Let's get Elena and that girl. It'll be easy.*

Humph.

We went to the training arena, and Estre came out of Ella. "C'mon, Pas. Lets duel." She grinned, and Pas came out of me. I stared at him. He did *not* seem ancient. Except for his eyes, that is. He looked like a fourteen year old boy, with long black hair, a slight tan, and grey eyes.

"What are you looking at?" He demanded.

I shook my head. "Nothing."

Pas opened his mouth, but Ella interrupted. "C'mon, Stren. Let's train."

Ella and I went to one end of the field, and Estre and Pas went to the other. Ella and I faced each other, and she drew her sword. She extended her free hand and summoned a fireball. I grinned and summoned a ball of water. She threw hers at me, and I threw mine to counter it. Unfortunately, mine got sucked into hers, and I cursed. I had to counter it before Ella said Bloccaggio. I used my amulet and found that there was an Earth core, a Water layer around it, a thin layer of air in storm form, and a fire covering. I sent it back at her, but I had let my MindBarriers weaken. Ella broke through and predicted my next move, which was to make the ball explode and knock her over, and then use a combination of Mist and Bloccaggio to capture her. Ella grinned. The ball exploded and knocked *me* over, and then she used mist and captured me using Bloccaggio. "Don't you have any imagination?" I grumbled.

"Plenty," she replied, grinning. "It just annoyed you more when I use your methods."

I scowled, and summoned some Mist. The capture didn't break, and I told Ella, "Free me, please."

"Freigabe." She gave me her hand, and I pulled her down. The next thing I remembered was lying on the ground on my stomach, with Ella's knee on my back. "Ha!" She said, and let me up.

"Remind me never to do that again," I said, wincing.

"Never do that again."

"Very funny."

"You need to work on doing the MindFights and Elemental magic simultaneously. Practice with Estre *and* Pas, got it?"

"Fine." I grumbled. Then I asked, "Why does Pas call Estre Elena?"

"That's her actual Elemental name."

"Why does one person need two names?" I groaned.

She raised her eyebrows and didn't answer. Instead, she said, "Let's see what Estre and Pas are doing." She walked away, and I had to run to catch up.

We reached the other end of the field (Big field), and what I saw... well, it was surprising to say the least.

They were moving really fast, their mouths and swords a blur. I heard a few random spells, like "Ontwapen!" and "Glissade". None of these spells made any kind of sense. They were very smooth in their movements, and they seemed to be floating in air. Finally, their Amulets got Empty, but that didn't stop them. They continued fighting with swords, and Estre summoned some Mist. Pas did the same, and there was a loud blast. Ella and I were knocked off our feet, and when I managed to get up, there was a crater sort of thing in between Estre and Pas, who has also been knocked of their feet. They grabbed each other's hand and Pulled themselves up. I saw them say some thing to each other, and they turned to us.

"How'd it go?" asked Estre.

"Fine," I replied.

"No, it didn't." Ella glared at me. "Stren here needs a *lot* of practice. Estre, Pas, would you help him when I go for my shifts?"

"Sure, Ella." They said at the same time, and I thought I saw them blush a bit.

They came back into us, and I asked, *A little crush, Monseigneur?*

Silence your tongue, boy.

Stop saying things in 'Old-New' speak.

What?

It's not 'silence your tongue'; it's 'shut up'.

Well, then, shut up.

I grinned. "Lets go, shall we?" I said, and headed towards the Magos Verdaderos.

"Not there, Stren." Said Ella, and went to the charging area.

I followed.

Chapter 7

Once we got out amulets recharged, Ella went to her shift. I went and trained with both Estre and Pas. Just great.

We followed Ella's recommendation for this session. Estre did the MindFights part, and Pas did the Elemental magic. I was pathetic at first, but I improved a lot. Pas and Estre didn't hold back, though, so I was never actually able to defeat them. After that, I went to my shift, and got bored for the next four hours.

⟶⟶≫⟶

Ella dragged me to the dueling area once we had finished, and Estre and Pas went away as usual. This time, most people went and watched Pas and Estre.

That was good news. No distractions.

Ella grinned. "Ready, dude?"

I grinned in response. "Yup."

She attacked, and this time, she didn't hold back (much). She did a MindAttack, and her sword flew at me at the same time. The sword was glowing so I sidestepped, and also strengthened my MindBarriers. She still broke through and I summoned armor made of Lutetium. The first attack she launched bounced off both my MindArmor and my real armor. The Lutetium of my real armor got a dent, and I realized that she had a Lutetium sword. I cursed, and did a complicated invisibility spell. I could therefore draw stuff, and she wouldn't know. Also, she couldn't detect me with her mind. I drew myself armour made of an enchanted metal that I had found before. I called it Lámpsi ánthi. It was a shiny and silver metal, and was easy to work with. However, once given a shape and cooled, it would not change shape.

I stopped the invisibility spell after donning the armor, and grinned at Ella. She was shocked when she saw my new armour. She yelled, "Katárgisi!" Remove. I didn't know how to stop it, and the armour flew off me. Ella whispered, "Katharíste Lámpsi ánthi." Cleanse Lámpsi ánthi. What did she mean, cleanse?

Some white mist went through the armor, but when it came out, it was grey. My heart went cold. The metal was Dark.

Ella turned to me, her kaleidoscopic eyes flashing. She attacked me so fast that I couldn't follow. She had disarmed me in a matter of seconds. She kept her sword at my neck. "Who gave you this?"

"What!?!" I exclaimed.

"Who gave you this metal, this armor?" She repeated, drawing some blood with her sword.

"No one gave it to me, I found it! I found that the metal was stronger than Lutetium, and I made myself a set of armor with it!" *And another thing,* I thought.

"I don't believe you." She said, her voice low. She attacked me with her mind, and I didn't last a second. I couldn't fight back since she took over my body, but even if she hadn't, I wouldn't have fought her anyway. *The metal- the metal is Dark! How is that even possible?* I felt that I couldn't even stop a feather floating down from touching me. Ella roughly searched my mind, and found the memory of me finding the metal.

I went back in time.

———◆———

I was walking down a narrow path, and tripped over something.
I looked down the path and found a piece of metal jutting out of the
ground.

"Flotteur en mi air," I whispered. The metal floated out of the
ground. It was really shiny, and I took a second to admire it. Then I ran
towards the forge (Yeah, camp has a forge), and started shaping it into
a sword. It was easy to forge, thankfully, and I let it cool after forming
the blade. I lifted the blade, and found it extremely light. There was a
voice telling me, *Lámpsi ánthi, Lámpsi ánthi, Lámpsi ánthi...*

"That's what the metal is," I said out loud. "Lámpsi ánthi." It fit
like a key in a lock. Then came the matter of naming the sword.

"Jaspis," I said. "Diamond." I smiled. Perfect.

I looked around, and found a bit more metal lying around. I made
sure I'd remember it, and took it with me to a little hiding place in the
Library room that Ella took me to.

The memory rippled, and Ella saw me as I had seen myself when
the Invisibility spell was still on. She saw me draw the armor, and then
withdrew from my mind.

———◆———

"Sano." She said, getting up. I rubbed my neck, feeling the little
cut heal. "Show me the sword."

I wordlessly drew it. "I'm so sorry. I didn't know that-"

"You ought to have checked." Ella snapped. I winced and looked
down, ashamed. "Katharíste Lámpsi ánthi."

After the blade was cleansed, the face of the metal rippled. The metal now had a gold color strip in the middle. Ella tried to hand the sword back to me, but I shook my head. "You purified it, you keep it."

"Don't be stupid," she growled. She threw it at me, and it went straight into its sheath, which was at my waist.

"Let's ask the blade." I suggested. I unbuckled my belt, and placed my right palm on the hilt. I looked at Ella, who shrugged and did the same.

"O opoíos eínai kýriós sias?" We said. Who is your master? The blade floated out of the sheath, and glowed briefly. When the glow faded, there were four identical swords. Two went to Ella, and two went to me.

We walked to the other end of the field, and it was pretty much like last time. Random spells, quick, smooth movements, etcetera, etcetera. Finally, Estre pulled of something unexpected, and yelled, "Kínisi!" I dunno what that means, but Pas shot back and slammed to the ground.

"You got me, Elena," said Pas.

"Well, of course!" Joked Estre, and went and pulled him up. Ella and I walked up to them, and they looked at us. Estre gasped, and Pas froze.

"Where did you get those?" Yelled both of them at the same time.

Ella and I shared our memories to Estre and Pas. They looked at us with seemingly newfound respect.

"Ella, Stren," Estre said. "You two are the Ones."

"What Ones?" Ella and I asked.

"The Ones who will defeat Malvagita Ubella and Cattiva Mauvaise once and for all."

Chapter 8

The ground became extremely quiet when Pas said that. There was a wind blowing, the kind that comes whenever I get shocked. Ella broke the silence.

"What!" She yelled, her black hair flying. "How can that be possible? Stren's training-"

"That may be," interrupted Estre. "But Stren is more powerful than Cattiva."

"I know." I said. "I had a dream the other night." I told them about that dream about Malvagita and Cattiva, his 'little apprentice'.

When I was done, Ella frowned and said, "So, Estre, Pas, does that mean that that – wait a moment." She turned to the rest of the Elementals, who had been watching this exchange silently. "The rest of you, go back to what ever it was you were doing before this little exchange." They grumbled and left. She waited till they left and resumed. "Does that mean that we *will* defeat Malvagita and Cattiva? We won't have to worry about defeat?"

"No, Ella," said Pas. "There's always a chance that you'll be defeated."

"What'll happen then?"

"You'll become like me," replied Estre.

"As in?"

"You'll never fade, never actually be able to actually *do* anything unless you have a host."

I wished I had never asked. Ella distracted me and said, "We'll do that anyway, right?"

"Yeah. You summoned the Pure form of White Magic."

Just then, Pas started disappearing, and Estre said urgently, "Pas! Stren! Quick!" Pas came back into me.

That was close, he said.

How so?

I was fading.

Those three words echoed in my mind. I realized that I had closed my eyes, and opened them. Estre went back into Ella, and we faced each other awkwardly.

"I'm sorry, Ella. I really, really am." I apologized again.

Ella took a deep breath. "Just be careful from now on." We walked in for a while, and Ella said, "I'm sorry I reacted so strongly. It's just… well, I trusted you." I noticed the past tense, and pointed it out to her. "I still do, but will you let me finish?"

"Sorry."

"Well, I trusted – sorry, trust – you, and then it seemed like you were Dark, that you were betraying my trust…I just felt so *angry*, so-"

"Ella," I interrupted. "I understand. I would have felt the same way, except I wouldn't have forgiven that easily. So, thank you."

We walked some more, and Ella asked, "Who's voice do you think it was?"

"No idea." I replied.

"Show me the memory again." She commanded. When I was done, she said, "We need to got to the Flower's place."

"Why?" I asked warily.

"'Cause that sounded a lot like Fiore Bluma."

Ella made me draw a bit of the impure metal, and showed it to Fiore when we got there. Of course, I didn't draw it in front of Fiore (Ella insisted on keeping this ability of mine a secret).

"Do you know what this is called?" Ella asked.

"Yeah, it's Lámpsi ánthi. It's our metal!" He grinned.

"What do you mean by 'our metal'?"

"We use it for most of our weapons. It literally means Flower metal. Why?"

"Can I see one weapon made of this?" She asked, ignoring the question.

"Sure, Ella." He drew his own blade.

Ella took a deep breath, and said, "Katharíste Lámpsi ánthi." Mist flowed through the metal and came out dark grey. Fiore drew a sharp breath.

"How…"

"I was hoping you'd be able to tell me." Ella said sharply.

"One sec." He sent a message to all the Flower Elementals, and gathered them to the living room. He invited us into the room, and everybody fell silent.

"Okay, all of you," Ella said. "Take out all the weapons made of Lámpsi ánthi."

The room was filled with murmurs, 'How does she know?' I smiled grimly to myself.

"Repeat after me." She was seriously doing a Magical lesson in the middle of all this! "Katharíste Lámpsi ánthi."

Every body said that, and the room was filled with light grey mist. Ella and I immediately summoned white mist, and so did Fiore. After 10 seconds, the Mist disappeared.

"Since when…" Ella began.

"Were you able to summon a Pure form?" I completed.

"Since my second day at camp." Fiore replied.

"Why didn't you tell us?" one of the other Elementals asked.

"It never came up."

Ella was eying Fiore suspiciously. She opened her mouth to say something, but I interrupted and said, "Okay, people. Next time you find some Lámpsi ánthi and forge it, remember to cleanse it." Then, I dragged Ella out of the room and we went to the Magos Verdaderos.

Chapter 9

"Why did you stop me?" Demanded Ella.

"He kept it a secret. He could have been the spy!"

"Why would he summon white mist? C'mon, Ella, relax." She scowled at me. I grinned. "Take a deep breath…Inhale…Exhawhoops!" The last part was because she had thrown a bit of mist at me. She probably said a spell, because it was chasing me around the room. "Ella! Stop – it – now!" I panted.

She was laughing hard, so it took some time before she said, "Mora!"

We both lay down on the ground, trying to regain our breath. When I finished, I said, "See? I can make you laugh even in the most serious of situations." I grinned, and ducked, as Ella threw a cushion on me (she was near a sofa).

"And I," She said, getting up. "Can make you train in the funniest of situations. You could have said Mora yourself." I groaned. "C'mon, get up."

She shot a fireball at me, and I yelped and rolled over. "Wasn't that unnecessary?"

"A bit, yeah. But it's your turn to clean the place up."

"Exactly!"

I would have ranted more, but our amulets started glowing just then. "A new Elemental." Ella beckoned me, and we 'teleported' to the Auditorium.

We planned some stuff, and waited for the new kid to arrive.

Stren! Ella! Stervia sent a panicked message. *We're under attack! The new Elemental – Malvagita and Cattiva are after her!*

Ella and I cursed simultaneously. *Where?* Ella asked.

North Petal of the outer flower. Pianta replied. *Stervia – down! Lau – Down! Hurry!*

I cursed, and grabbed Ella's hand. We 'teleported' to the 'north petal'.

When we got there, only two of the rest of the Seven were standing (Pianta and Cielo), and they were weakening. We stepped in, and the balance shifted. The new girl was dodging some wisps of black mist, and the others were helping her. I sent two tendrils of White magic, one towards the Black magic, and one towards Cattiva. I directed my Magic towards the second tendril, and yelled, "Bloccaggio!" The mist captured Cattiva, and cut off his Magical influence. I turned my attention towards Malvagita, and I did not like what I saw.

Pianta and Cielo were down, and Ella had some pretty bad cuts.

"Go, help her," croaked Pianta.

I needed no further incentive.

I sent an all Elements + Mist ball at Malvagita, and whispered, "Sýllipsi." The ball captured Malvagita, and merged with the one with Cattiva. Ella collapsed, and pushed herself up.

"The others?"

"No idea."

That answer got some energy into her. She walked shakily towards me, and we went to each of the seven, healing them. At the end of the trip, Ella collapsed. Estre came out of her immediately, and said, "Sanare." All the cuts disappeared, and Estre went back into Ella. I turned to my little hitch-hiker.

Thanks for the help. I said sarcastically.

You're welcome. He didn't get the sarcasm, and I told him so. *I did help. Who do you think gave you all that energy?*

I gave up trying to converse with him, and concentrated on giving some of my energy to the rest of the seven and getting them to stand on their own feet. When they did, we all turned to the new girl.

She was about twelve years old, and had short brown hair. She had a medium tan. I looked into her eyes, which were golden. I gasped.

"Sorella?" I asked.

The girl started. "Stren?" She walked towards me, and asked, "Is it really you?"

"Of course it's me," I said, a grin spreading across my face. "Who else could it be?"

"Uh, Stren?" Interrupted Selena. "Who is this?"

I turned to the Seven. "Sorella, these are my friends, Ella, Pianta, Cielo, Lau, Selena, and Stervia. Guys, this is Sorella, my sister."

Chapter 10

"Your…sister." Lau forced the words out.

I nodded, and turned to Sorella. "Why were they chasing you?"

"It's a long story."

"I'm-"

"Stren!" Ella interrupted. "Let's find out what kind of Elemental she is?"

I cursed myself internally. "Yeah. C'mon, sis."

"Don't call me sis!"

I grinned. Just like old times.

——◆——

We walked to the Auditorium. Throughout the way there, I was arguing with Ella about the arrangements we had made to introduce the Elemental Amulets. Finally, Ella said, "Stren, you *will* do it. Stop arguing. Your sister is looking at us weirdly." I shut up and cursed mentally.

We finally settled in the auditorium, and I waved my hand dramatically. A cloth covering a set of Amulets moved away, and I was thinking, *Not Elementa, not Elementa…*

She got the Fire amulet. I announced it to the people, "Sorella Le Feu, Fire."

"Sorella Majier." She corrected.

"That's exactly what your brother said when we called him Stren Elementa." Ella said, grinning.

"Le Feu is your Elemental name. I'll explain."

"The rest of you," Ella said. "Back to your normal activities!" Then she turned to me. "Take Sorella around camp and Explain stuff to her." She grinned. "If your sister is anything like you, then you should know how Juliet and I felt on your first day. I," She said, forestalling my protest. "Will check on those two."

I felt guilty. "I'll come along. You don't mind, do you Sorella?"

"I'll come as well." She replied.

"No!" Ella and I said at the same time. "It's too dangerous." Ella said. "They are very powerful."

"My brother's spells will hold." She said with absolute confidence. I started grinning.

"Don't be so sure." Ella said. "I was able to break his defenses easily when we were training."

Sorella smiled sweetly. "I'll come."

Ella started to agree, but I intervened. "No, Sorella, it's too dangerous. Selena?" I called. "Take Sorella to the Fire place, and do *not* listen to anything she says. Put a spell to make her keep quiet or something."

I dragged Ella away, while Sorella started saying, "That's not-"

Selena cast the spell.

———❈———

We went to the North Petal and cleared everybody out of it.

"Okay, Ubella." Ella's voice was filled with a kind of loathing, which I had never heard before. "Where are the leaders?"

"Oh, just outside camp, waiting for my orders."

"No more riddles." I said.

"Oh, it's not a riddle; it's a fact." Cattiva said.

"Shut up, Mauvaise, I wasn't talking to you." He shut up immediately.

"Where – exactly – are the leaders?" Ella asked again.

Malvagita smiled. "I'll show you." He burst the Elemental cage with a little bit of Black mist, and grabbed Ella's hand. Cattiva burst out of his place, and grabbed my hand. He touched the burn, the world spun around me.

Suddenly, I was standing outside Camp, and the leaders had a black - well, a black something – around their amulet. They were standing exactly as it was on my amulet, with Juliet standing in the middle. Their amulets were constantly getting charged, and this was leaking out to a little black ball. I whispered, "Vlépo." It means See in Prima Lingua. The little ball didn't seem so little now. There was so much energy in it, and that energy was leaking towards camp. I followed it, and it was leaking into...Malvagita. But there was a light stream going into Ella as well. Nothing went into me, however. The world spun again, and I found myself in the North Petal (again). I shoved Cattiva back, and Ella shoved Malvagita out. We (Ella and I) stood back-to-back, with me facing Cattiva and Ella facing Malvagita. Pas advised me.

Look at him. Find out what his weaknesses are.

A little help?

Look at his eyes. He is afraid of you, or rather, of your power.

What!

You are *more powerful than him, are you not?*

145

Well, yeah, but-

No buts. Then, look at his stance. Try to predict what kind of move he'll do.

I looked at him, and he seemed to have a kind of defense position, but looking at his hand, I could tell he was going to hurl a spell at me (or Ella) the second I moved forward. Then, I looked at his other hand, and saw that his knife was in defense position. I told Pas my observations, and he seemed to be a bit pleased. However, he said, *Look at his overall stance. What does it look like?*

I looked at him, and saw that he had shifted slightly, and was ready to attack. His stance was also slightly on the defensive side, which meant he would be prepared if I attacked first.

I decided to surprise him, and twitched my sword arm. He threw a spell at me, and I said, "Stamatíste!" Stop! The spell stopped in mid air. "Vade!" Go! The spell shot back at him, and hit him square on the chest. He stumbled and disappeared, and I felt a searing pain in my chest. I doubled over and blacked out.

Chapter 11

When I woke up, I was lying down on soft grass, and was clutching the sheath of one of the Lámpsi ánthi swords. I released it, and found my swords missing. I started panicking, when someone came and said, "Calm down, Stren. They're right here." It was Ella. I counted back from twenty, took three deep breaths, and calmed down.

"Where – Where are we?" I asked. It looked like a forest, and there was a little lake beside us.

"Outside Camp."

"Gee, really?" I asked sarcastically.

"I don't know, exactly. I just let Estre direct us."

"Well, ask her!"

"I did."

I dropped the subject, and asked, "Why are we here?"

She turned away. "They took over camp."

I waited a moment for the information to sink in. Then I took a shaky breath and asked, "How?"

"After you passed out, Malvagita attacked, and I was losing energy. I took some from you, and got all the sub – leaders and the Seven here."

I felt myself panicking again. "What about Sorella?"

"Dude," A new voice said. It was Sorella. "I happen to be the substitute leader for the Fire Elementals."

"Oh," I said. "Yeah, I knew that."

Sorella snorted. I changed the subject. "So, none of the Seven are Subs?"

"Except me."

"So that's 9 substitute leaders, plus the Seven, so that's 16 people, against the two most evil dudes in the world. I think the odds are in our favor!" I grinned.

"You forgot something." Ella said softly.

"What?"

"The Leaders."

I remembered what Cattiva and Malvagita showed me. "So, they have a lot of energy. Thirteen against 16. Still in our favor."

She smiled a little. "Well, Let's get planning. Get up!"

I groaned, and Sorella asked in concern, "You OK?"

"Yeah, He's fine." Ella said. "He always does that whenever I tell him to get up and do some work."

Sorella glared at me. "You are so lethargic!"

"Enough with the big words, already!" I said.

Ella interrupted a potential fight, and said, "Okay, I'll fill you in on which Elementals are here. There is a Fire, Sorella, two Suns, Helios and Selena, Two moons, Máni and Lau, two plants, Antheia and Pianta, a flower, Fiore, a Rainbow, Arcus, two stones, Karus and Stervia, one Animal, Leon, and two stars, Astrum and Cielo. Also, two Elementas, You and I."

"So, Sorella, Helios, Selena, Máni, Lau, Antheia, Pianta, Fiore, Arcus, Karus, Stervia, Leon, Astrum, Cielo, you, and I. Any Idea about what's going on in camp?"

"Nope."

I tried not to get too annoyed. "Did you try that earth thingy?"

"Yeah. Didn't work."

"Then How do we get to camp?"

"The same way those two did. We walk in."

"No Magic?"

"No magic."

An idea began forming at the back of my mind, and I jumped up, reached into my pocket and grabbed a pencil and paper (Hey, you never know), and drew a diamond. It was about three inches long. I drew a shaft for a spear, and attached it to the diamond with a quick spell. I made the spear shaft hollow, with two layers. I filled the inner layer with mist and put a spell so that it would never run out. Then, I told Ella to duplicate it, and she did. I took the original and made 7 more duplicated. Ella did the same to the other one. Then, we called the others to the place (Sorella was training with Stervia). I gave each of them a spear.

"Okay, do you see an empty hollow area in the shaft?" They replied in affirmative. "Fill it with your Element's Magical essence." Magical essence was a form of their magic, the stuff that came to their Amulet when they charged their Amulets. They did that, except Ella and I. "Now cast a spell to make sure it doesn't get depleted." They did that. Then I went around and sealed it such that the Magic or Mist came out whenever the wielder wished. I explained it to them and then sent them back to train. Then I turned to Ella. How do we do it for us?"

"Divide the thing into 12 compartments. Fill it the same way it is in the Amulet." We finished it, and started training. This time, Pas stayed in me, and Estre stayed in Ella. We trained for some time (I still couldn't beat Ella!), and then slept.

Chapter 12

We went on a fixed schedule for a few days, consisting of training, planning, eating, and sleeping. We were planning to send a group of two or three fighters to each of the five petals, concealed by invisibility spells, with one of the Seven in each of the groups. Ella and I were to go to the North Petal and draw Cattiva and Malvagita out. The groups were as follows:

Group I.   Pianta, Sorella
Group II.   Cielo, Helios, Karus
Group III. Selena, Máni, Arcus
Group IV.   Lau, Antheia, Leon
Group V.   Stervia, Fiore, Astrum
Group VI.   Ella, Stren

So, we made some Communication devices (Lot of help from Pas and Estre), and made a strong plan (I thought it was strong, at least.). Groups I, II, III, IV, and V were to go to the five petals invisibly, and Group VI was to Approach the North Petal visibly and lure Cattiva and Malvagita out. I asked Ella how we'd do it, but she just said, "Leave it to me." She seemed extremely worried, but that didn't stop her from beating me every time we trained.

"How do you keep doing it?" I asked after a particularly humiliating defeat.

"'Concentration."

"What's that supposed to mean?" I asked (yelled, actually).

"You get distracted!" She responded with an equally loud tone. "You let your Emotions get the best of you! I feel the color of your thoughts when we train, and seriously, you ought to be ashamed. You keep thinking, 'Oh, she's not going to get past this.' That thought distracts you, and your defenses go down."

"Well, what can I do!?!" I half yelled, half screamed.

"First thing in keeping your emotions in check is shutting up." I scowled, but I shut up. "Then, you relax." I started protesting (How can I relax in the middle of a war?), but Ella raised her hand and said, "Shut up." I tried relaxing, but it didn't work.

"No can do." I said.

She grinned and said, "Remember this conversation? 'Take a deep breath...Inhale...Exhale...'" I grinned in spite of myself. I followed her steady rhythm, and felt myself relaxing. "Next step, clear your mind. Stop thinking of things that make you angry, sad, resentful...Just calm down."

I thought. I was angry with Malvagita and Cattiva for dragging my sister into this; I was resentful that she never got proper training. Ella wanted me to let go of that? She seemed to realize what I was thinking, because she said, "You cannot let you emotions get the best of you. Your anger at those two is understandable, but you need to know who he is, what his weaknesses are. You need not forgive or forget; you just need control. Clear your mind, now." I tried and heard Ella's voice, "Ready?" I nodded.

She attacked with both mind and sword at the same time, but I was ready. I parried her sword thrust, and sent a counter attack. I also kept her out of my mind, and I tried to attack her as well. Her eyes narrowed, and she sent her sword point first. I tried to block it, and caught my sword under her hilt. She twisted hers, and the sword clattered away. *How?* I wondered for a moment, confused. That was all she needed. She got past my defenses and overpowered me. She withdrew a second later, and I stepped back. "How?" I asked out loud.

She grinned. "You got my sword under your hilt, but you didn't disarm me. Our swords are the same length, so I got my sword on your hilt. Then, I just had to twist my blade, and *voilà,* one disarmed opponent."

"Lets try that again." I said. This time, every time she sent her blade point first, I just sidestepped. Finally, we had locked our blades and were swaying, trying to get an advantage. Suddenly, Ella dropped her sword and clutched her arm. A moment later, I felt a searing pain on my arm. I collapsed clutched my arm. a second later, I realized that the Burn that I had on my hand was – well, burning. I quickly summoned some white mist and covered my burn with it. I glanced at Ella. She was lying down on her back with her eyes closed. As I was looking, a cut formed on her chest. I scrambled up and immediately collapsed as another wave of pain washed over me. I yelled, "Somebody! We need a healer!" I felt a pressure building on my MindBarriers, and I readied myself for a MindFight, with pure Lámpsi ánthi armor and sword. I strengthened the barriers and held my sword in front of me. After some time, the pressure reduced and disappeared. I realized my burn was glowing, and I removed the mist from it slightly. After about two seconds, it stopped glowing. I removed the mist completely, and glanced at Ella. Nobody had responded to my call, so I walked to her myself. I whispered, "Sanare." The cut healed, and she opened her eyes. I glared at her. "Explain."

She smiled weakly. "Some water first, if you don't mind."

I got her some water, and she told me what happened. Apparently, Malvagita and Cattiva attacked her with their minds, and she was dazed. Her arm was killing her (Not literally), and she was in no shape to fight. She tried to summon Lutetium armor, but Cattiva cut her short with a few cuts on her hand. Then, Malvagita came in, and while she was repeatedly cut off mid-spell, she got a cut on her chest. Malvagita was about to take over, when Estre, who had previously been doing god knows what, came to the rescue. She (Estre) cut Malvagita on the chest and Cattiva on the arm, and sent them both out. Then, Ella felt the cut healing, and woke up.

After finishing this narration, She glanced at her arms. I glanced there too, and saw a lot of small cuts there. I scowled mentally. "Sanare." I said, and healed her cuts.

"Thanks." She smiled. She tried to get up, and immediately fell down.

"C'mon, let's get you to the tent."

"No!" She said fiercely.

I sighed. "Ells-"

"Don't call me that!"

I sighed again. "Ella, you need rest. You trained a ton, you fought those two, and you expect to train more and plan after that?"

"It's not that. Pianta and Cielo."

I understood immediately. Pianta and Cielo must have been attacked as well.

I hesitated. "Fine, but after that, you're sleeping."

She huffed. "Fine."

I grinned. "Say that in Prima Lingua."

"Quod."

153

"I didn't tell you to say 'that'," I said, making quotation marks, "In Prima Lingua, I told you to swear that you will sleep immediately after we check on Pianta and Cielo and make sure they're alright."

She scowled. "Dórmiam post nos facio certus Pianta et Cielo sunt licuit."

I smiled and helped Ella up. We then walked to the general training area.

Chapter 13

When we got there, we saw everybody standing around Pianta and Cielo with their eyes closed. Ella and I closed our eyes and reached into their minds. They had joined their minds and were fighting Malvagita and Cattiva.

It was not a fair fight.

Malvagita and Cattiva were winning.

"Thought you were temporarily out of action?" Malvagita said when he saw Ella.

She didn't deign that with a reply. Instead, she said, "Stren, Cover me. Katharó Lámpsi Anthí panoplía, to spathiá." She got a set of pure Lámpsi ánthi armor and two swords. I summoned a few arrows and a bow and shot them at Malvagita and Cattiva. They disappeared.

We withdrew from each other's mind. Ella and I went and healed the others numerous cuts and bruises. Then we approached Pianta and Cielo.

"How do you do it?" Cielo demanded.

"Do what?" I asked.

"Get them out of your head." Pianta said.

"Well," I began. Ella interrupted, thank god. I had no Idea what to say.

"We'll teach you tomorrow. Are you guys OK?"

"Yeah."

"Great," I said, grinning. "Then, you can go and sleep." I told Ella.

"No."

I grinned even more. "You swore."

She grinned back. "You see, I only swore to sleep after we checked on Pianta and Cielo. I didn't swear to sleep immediately after that. So, technically, even if I sleep later tonight, I'm not breaking my oath."

I scowled. "You and your technicalities."

She grinned cheekily. "I guess you'll pay me back?" She asked teasingly.

"Shut up."

"In fact, I think you have to pay me back – how many times, exactly? Hmm, let's see, there was that time while planning, when I sent some whi-" She cut off, and her eyes widened. "Oh no. Oh no. This is not happening. Katarómai!" She ran off.

There was a short silence, which Pianta and Cielo broke at the same time. "Katarómai?"

I grinned hesitantly. "Curse word. Let's just say it's meaning is similar to Maldita."

Their eyebrows shot up. "Let's catch up with her," Suggested Cielo. "Something must be up, what with her using such language."

"Gee, you think?" I asked, sarcastically.

"One moment, Stren Majier."

I turned and came face-to-face with my sister.

"Hey, 'La. 'Sup?"

"First of all, stop calling me 'La. My name is *Sorella*. Secondly, what on Earth is going on?"

"To answer your question, a little later, please? Also, It's not just Stren Majier (If you're trying to be intimidating, that is), it's Stren Majier Elementa."

"Swear it."

"What?" I said, pretending to be confused. She glared at me. "Fine. I swear to explain later."

"Immediately after you finish talking to Ella now?"

"Yes, Sorella."

She walked off. I turned, and saw Ella walking back. "What's wrong?"

"A lot. Come on. Pas, we need your help."

Pas- I began.

I heard, you know. I am not deaf.

I bit my tongue to prevent myself from responding, 'Dude, you have no ears. You're dead.' He probably would have said something like, 'yes, so if I cannot hear what she said, then you are deaf.'

I went to our tent and saw our plan. "We're wasting our amulets' charge, you know."

"I may be a magician, but I do not have the ability to summon a good planning board."

I pursed my lips. "Well, then, it's no good asking someone who actually can, is it?" I asked sarcastically.

"Oh, yeah…" She said, comprehension dawning on her face. I snorted. "Pas," she continued. "Can you show Stren what Camp looks like? Make him know enough about its structure to draw us a planning board?"

Pas didn't answer. Instead, he shared some of his memories. I suddenly got a very good look at camp. I pulled a twig out of the ground, and started drawing. I put the twig down some five minutes later, and got up. It took a minute, but there came a super-cool planning board, complete with the pins for the Seven and the substitute leaders. There were even those Walls that I had drawn on my first day here (Long story).

Did you get that info from me?

No. I get it automatically thanks to my position as Custos Cartis.

I grinned. Now, we had a chance.

Chapter 14

We stayed there all evening, and finally came up with a plausible plan. It's practically impossible to explain it without the board, but I'll give it my best shot.

With Pas's help, we found out how exactly we need to bypass the Borders we had put up. Basically, we could use the All Elements thingy we had summoned the other day (Long story). The others had to go in via their cabins, since they had their Element in the ceiling or something. After that, we had to cast invisibility spells (Some intricate White spell in Prima Lingua), and sneak out to the Central Wall. Then, Pas and Estre would lend us their strength, and we would sink the Lutetium into the ground. Then, if that didn't get Malvagita's attention (Not that we were trying to do that, we just needed the space), we would send out Elements' essence (The stuff we filled in the spears) from the spears. It would form a ball of Elemental Magic. Then, Estre and Pas would come out partly, completely invisible. Estre would send a ball of white Magic, and then the 16 of us (Living Magicians) would start a spell and cleanse the Camp of all Dark Magic. We had to finish the spell, and stop Malvagita and Cattiva. So, we had to help Estre and Pas increase their strength. So, Ella and I were practicing Magic by using both theirs and our magic. Estre was already the equivalent of 8 Magicians. Pas was 6. So, I had to do it more than Ella.

The spell the 16 of us had to do was complex, and we could say it out loud only once. The pressure was astounding, and we were reading the spell as many times as we could.

Finally, Pas and Estre's magic was the equivalent of 12 and 13 Magicians respectively. We got everybody around, and told him or her that.

The attack had begun.

Chapter 15

The first part of the plan went perfectly. We got to Camp no problem, and sunk the central defense wall. No one was there, and Malvagita didn't seem notice. Then, Ella nodded (We were able to see her because we had the same invisibility spell), and we brought out the spears. We let the tips touch, and released the Magic. A colorful ball rose out from the tips, and went high above our heads. We resisted the urge to turn and look out for Malvagita and Cattiva. We joined our minds, and waited for Estre to send the mist.

Estre, I heard Ella say. *It doesn't matter if he's not here. Send the Mist.*

Estre came out, and shimmered, as though she were a mirage. Then, the illusion stopped, and she sent the mist towards the ball. The moment it connected, we started our spell.

I heard the others say the spell, but I concentrated on keeping pace, making sure I didn't slip, and little things like that. "…The power spreads, and sends purity in all directions. The Darkness in the Haven leaves…" The spell goes on like that for some time, and I was starting to get tired. Estre and Pas supplied some more strength, and we were soon saying the final line.

"Máio to skotádi emás afísei gia pánta!" Let the Darkness leave this place forever! The ball of Magic exploded in a blast of white magic, but we held our ground. We held our spears close, and turned to face the rest of Camp. There was a little disturbance in the north, but it disappeared soon enough. Soon, the whole Camp was cleansed, but there was still no sign of Malvagita and Cattiva.

Ella yelled, "Come on, White Elementals, to the currently non-existent central wall!"

We waited for two minutes, and they all came. "Are you all OK?" Ella asked.

Somebody ran forward. "Ella!" It was Apprendista. She tackled Ella in a hug, and would have impaled herself on the spear had Ella not thrown it to me. I caught it, and Ella held Apprendista at arms length. "How are you? You look dead tired. You all do." Ella said.

Apprendista launched into the story. After we left, the sky had turned black, and Malvagita and Cattiva took over camp. The campers, of course, went into rebellion, and were going good till three days before, when Malvagita created something that they couldn't see too clearly, but Apprendista told us in an undertone that she thought it was a Dark army. Of course, she thought that it got destroyed. Lot of the Elementals had given up, and had been doing nothing in the 'rebellion'. Apprendista, Kleur, and Allia led the other Elementals, and were going to sneak out of Camp.

Ella scowled at the last part. "You couldn't do anything more dangerous, could you?" She asked sarcastically.

"Nope!" Apprendista replied cheerfully. Ella smiled and shook her head. a second later, the smile faded, and she asked, "The leaders?"

Apprendista shook her head. "They were in the auditorium, but they disappeared as soon as the Spell started taking effect. Allia checked."

"Malvagita and Cattiva?"

"They fled as soon as you sunk the wall."

Ella scowled more. "Do you think it was a coincidence, the leaders disappearing as soon as the spell started?"

"What do you mean?" Asked a girl standing at Apprendista's left. Alia, I guessed.

"Never mind." Ella shook her head. She glanced at her arm, probably checking if the burn was still there. It was. "Any idea why these haven't gone yet?"

They shook their head.

"I have something, but it's unlikely." I turned, and saw Sorella. "They may have used, um, white magic in those burns."

I turned to Ella, who's expression was unfathomable. I shrugged. "Maybe."

Ella turned to the Elementals. "We need to get the leaders back. We need to go into an even more intense training schedule. The sixteen of us," She said, indication to us. "Will help you all learn the other little things, like MindFights, Prima lingua, and other little stuff. We will get them back. Helios, Mani, Antheia, Fiore, Arcus, Karus, Leon and Astrum will teach their fellow Elementals. The seven of us," She said, indicating to the Seven, "will teach you anything extra we find. We will train together for an hour everyday. Let's start."

We went to the training area, and trained.

Chapter 16

Nothing much happened that week. We just trained, and trained, and trained. Ella and Pas got together for one-and-a-half hours and made a spell to keep Malvagita and Cattiva out for a good two months. Then, they made me draw a bigger model of Camp, and we made teams by assessing each individual camper. We got eight teams of twenty campers each, with Ella and I going to whichever place needed us the most. Sorella would stay with us (Ella and I), thank goodness.

One night, I had a weird dream. Yes, again. I saw Pas, who wordlessly grabbed my hand and took me to a Dark place. I saw Malvagita and Cattiva, standing near a model of camp. I realized that it was our old model. They seemed tobe planning something. I whispered, "Akoúso." Hear.

"...Send the army-" Cattiva was saying.

"And then what? We need the boy and the girl. Stren and Ella."

"We can instruct them."

"Will you?"

"Yes."

Cattiva started rising from the chair, but Malvagita said, "Stop. I say we go with the Skión, lead them."

"When, Duchë?"

Malvagita grinned at the title (Duchë means Master, or leader.). "Tomorrow, as soon as the sun sets. It is the winter solstice, when Darkness is greatest. It will be…Perfect."

The dream faded, and I woke up with a start. *Did you just show me that?* I demanded. *Are they actually planning to attack tomorrow night?*

Yes.

I threw off the covers and got to Ella's bed. "Ella, WAKE UP!" I yelled.

She shot up. "What happened, did they attack? Did a new camper come? Did-"

I interrupted. "I had a dream." She threw a water-ball at me, which I stopped. "Listen, Katarómai Vobis! Just listen! They're going to attack tomorrow, as soon as the sun sets!"

Ella sat there stunned for a moment. Then, "What! Out! Afíste!" I flew out of the room and into the hall. I went to my room, and changed into something somewhat presentable. Then, I went and banged on Ella's door. "Are you coming or what?"

She threw the door open in a second, and pulled me to the planning room. "Do you know when and how?"

"Malvagita and Cattiva plan on leading the Skión here themselves. What are Skión?"

Ella cursed under some breath. "Dark shadows. They could be called small scale Anima Tueurs."

"As hard to dispatch?"

"No, thankfully. We need to train the Campers differently now. They need to learn to fight with their minds and Elements at the same time. They need to be able to fight something that has the power of illusion."

"How do we teach them in time?"

She didn't answer. Instead, she touched her communications stone, and a moment later, the Seven and the substitute leaders came. "They're going to attack tomorrow as soon as the sun sets. Cancel all activities today, and get all the Elementals to the Auditorium. They have Skión." Then, she gave the substitute leaders a communication stone. "I took the liberty of duplicating mine. It's a communication stone. That will probably be very useful. Let's go!" All the Elementals went to the auditorium. Seconds later, the Elementals appeared. While they settled down, Pianta and Cielo came and stood on Ella's left, but one and two steps back respectively. I took the hint and stepped back as well. The other 12 completed the formation, with Selena and Lau next to me, Stervia next to Cielo, and the other nine on either side. Ella looked a little uncomfortable with this, and pulled me forward, so that both of us were at the head. Then, she waited for precisely five seconds, and yelled, "Ruhe!" Everybody shut up. "Sprechen Sie." She explained (Again) that Malvagita and Cattiva were attacking the next day. Then, without letting anyone start talking, she continued, setting a firm schedule for everybody. "Get started." She finished the speech. "Stren, take the Animal Elementals. If you need me, I'll be with the Rainbows. Sorella will be with you. Let's go. Arcus, lead the way." They left.

I glanced at Sorella. "C'mon, Sorella, Leon. Lets go to the Animal Elementals." We left.

———✦———

We trained harder than we ever had before, and that is saying something. We trained at every spare moment that we had. We shifted our training area to the charging area. Once, in the middle, I approached Ella, who in the middle of a duel with Estre.

"Mýga!" Ella yelled, and flew up. Estre was after her in a second, but Ella had dome something unexpected. She quickly disarmed Estre and placed her sword at Estre's neck. "Ntáoun." They landed, and I went in closer.

"I had the Elementals split into groups of four and practice. I think it's time for me to do some training." I told Ella.

She blew her hair out of her eyes, and said, "Sure, but wait a moment." She closed her eyes for a second, and opened them again.

"With the ancients or without?" She enquired.

"With. It'll help increase their power."

"C'mon, then. Let's fight."

I drew my swords, and so did Ella. We circled each other for ten seconds. Ella Struck first. She yelled, "Elementis!" The twelve Elements circled her swords. She pointed one of them at me, and a ball of the Elements flew at me.

"Tueri!" I yelled, and the ball stopped in mid air and burst. "Apergías!" Ella was knocked back, but she landed on her feet. She leapt forward, and slashed her swords. I yelped and jumped back, falling down. A smoky 'X' burned in front of me. A voice yelled, "Páno!" My swords flew up and out of my reach. "Katásvesi tis." I glanced up, and saw Ella place her now cold swords at my neck. "Give up?" She asked.

"Definitely." I gulped. She helped me up.

"Don't be afraid to imitate your enemy. You could have blocked my swords after I enchanted them if you had yourself. You just have to make sure the spell isn't Dark." She advised. "Now, get back to the Animal Elementals!"

I left.

Chapter 17

I lost track of what happened after that. About seven-thirty in the night, Ella shouted, "Stop!" Everybody put down his or her weapon/s. "We can call it a day. You all did great. All of you, go ask your substitute leader for a communication stone. It looked some thing like this," she held out her own, "but it'll be in a different color. Come here at seven-thirty. You cannot afford to be late. Good job, everybody." Everybody left, but Ella stayed back. I walked up to her, and asked, "Coming?"

"Yeah. I'll just clear this mess up." She murmured a spell, and turned to me. "Okay, let's go."

We walked in silence. I went to my room and fell asleep as soon as my head hit the pillow.

When I woke up, it was five thirty in the morning, and still dark. I decided to go to Ella's room and see if she was up. Her bed was empty, like she'd never slept on it. Her table was messed up. *She must have stayed up late planning, and fallen asleep at her desk,* I guessed.

I went out, and saw Ella standing at Rhea point. I walked up to her. "Hey," I said.

She whirled round, her hand on the hilt of one of her swords, which was half drawn. She saw me standing there, and relaxed. "Oh, it's you," she said, sheathing her sword. "Hi." She turned around again, and gazed absently into the horizon.

"What's wrong, Ella?" I asked. She shook her head. "Tell me." I told her.

She took a deep breath. "I'm just worried. What if I'm wrong, and the plan fails? I don't think I can stand it if – if we – if we lose anyone. It's just-" She shook her head. "I don't want to be responsible for anyone's death." She said.

I moved in closer. She stiffened, and then relaxed. "Don't think that way," I said. "We will stop those two, and get the leaders back. It'll be absolutely fine."

She took a deep breath, and relaxed. "Thanks, Stren." She straightened up. "Well, we need to get going. It won't do for us to be late, now, will it?"

I told her, "Race you to the recharge area!"

She didn't even reply, but just took off. I ran hard just to keep up, but she seemed to be taking a jog in the park, except she was really fast. She didn't go any faster, though, and we went to the charging area at the same time. "Draw?" She asked. I nodded, trying to catch my breath without letting her notice. She noticed, however, and said, "Here." She placed her hand on my chest, and felt energy flow into me.

"Thanks." I told her.

"Don't mention it." We waited a minute, and Ella said, "Let's train while we're waiting, shall we?"

I nodded, though it wasn't really a question. I jumped up, and grabbed my swords. "Ready?" I asked. She nodded. I attacked her first, whispering, "Tachýtita." My pace quickened, but Ella, surprisingly, blocked it. I attacked again, but Ella caught the blow with the flat of one of her blades, and spun it, sending one of my swords out of my hand. I grasped the other tightly, and whispered, "Elementa." The blade glowed with power, and I struck. Amazingly, Ella blocked it, holding both her swords parallel to each other. She whispered something else, and I flew back. I managed to land on my feet, and I pointed my sword at her. She said something, and one of her swords transformed into a shield. I whispered, "Vlépo." I saw her sword and shield glowing with an enormous amount power. She attacked, and I caught her blow on my sword. I reached out with my mind, and met with her MindBarriers. I thought, *Conteram.* The barriers shattered, and I went in. Immediately, Ella's mind self surrounded me, and took control. She forced me to drop my sword, and stayed for a second. When she withdrew, I noticed the place had become quite full. Ella told me, "Don't attack with your mind if you know, or suspect, that your opponent is more powerful than you. I have the upper hand as Estre is within me, and she is pretty powerful. You should wait until your opponent attacks, in which case you can perform magic, and he or she can't. Okay?" I nodded, and picked up my swords. I started removing the spell, but Ella stopped me. "It is to you advantage if your opponent does not know what magic your weapon contains." I nodded, and went to the Animal Elementals. We started training.

Chapter 18

We went on training, breaking only for lunch. When it was an hour to sundown, Ella broke up training, but told us not to leave the charging area. She called the Seven, and we created a single sphere that would charge only amulets that are predominantly White. Ella found a way to shrink it and slipped it into her pocket. Then we went back to the charging area (We had gone out while doing this). A few minutes later, Ella told us to put on our armor. She also taught them a spell, so that they could protect themselves from most attacks. We all put on the armor, and Ella yelled, "Seven, Leaders, Formation!" We got into the same formation as we had in our previous trip to the Auditorium. Then Ella stepped forward, and gave a little speech, encouraging everyone to fight like they'd done while training, and telling them that they'd win if they'd fight loyally for the White, and so on, and so forth.

When she stepped back, she pushed me forward a bit, and told me with her MindSpeech to give a speech myself. I don't remember exactly what I said, but I remembered Ella whispering, "Good speech."

I just nodded, being too nervous to speak.

It'll be fine, kid. I gave a start. I'd forgotten about Pas, since he'd been so quiet for so long.

Probably. I said, not really paying attention to him. He seemed to realize what was going on.

Sorella will be fine. I didn't react, so he dropped the subject. Instead, he gave me more spells, and told me exactly what to do when someone attacks, and – well, he basically gave me some last minute training.

"Okay, Elementals," Ella said. "It's five minutes to sundown. Form!" She turned to face the North exit, and the Rainbow Elementals went behind her. I went to the South exit, with the Animal Elementals and Sorella behind me. I vaguely heard the other Elementals get into formation. Ella yelled, "Move out!" We moved out. The Sun went down a minute we reached the area we were supposed to be defending. A second later, Ella sent me a MindMessage. *They are attacking the North group. Ámyna, do your jobs. Everyone else, come to the North group.*

"Nótio mé, Move north! Do not break formation! I repeat, do not break formation! Move!" We did a quick march to the north, and saw that two other groups had already reached. "Archers, do you have a clear shot?" I shouted.

"We might be able to shoot the Skión in back there, but it will make no difference," an archer replied. I nodded, and yelled, "Group Fire, plan 5!" That meant they had to go flying in invisible. "Group Rainbow, Plan 3!" They had to go visibly on foot from the left. "Group Colors, plan 6!" They had to go on foot invisibly from the right. The groups left.

"What about us, Stren?" A girl asked. The last group was Group Elementis.

"Group Elementis," I said, softly, with both mind and mouth. "Plan one." The Elementals grasped their weapons tighter, and muttered the invisibility spells. We had to go and attack head on, since the battle was going bad for the North group. It was the most dangerous plan we had formulated, but it was necessary. Fortunately, this group contained only the most competent fighters. We altered our formation, and I yelled, "Attack!" We charged forward. I destroyed as many Skión as possible, and found Ella. She was fighting Cattiva and Malvagita. I slashed down three more Skión, and tried to go help Ella. Something blocked me, and I staggered back. Suddenly, the shadows at my feet shifted and rose, and I walked back slowly. *Not that, please not that...*I silently pleaded.

The shadows solidified, and became a humanoid figure. It was over ten feet tall, and held a black staff in its hand, and wore a black cloak. I looked up.

A cold fist seemed to clench my heart.

Looking down at me through those Dark black eyes was an Anima Tueur.

Chapter 19

The battle raged around me. I ignored it.

I closed my eyes, and focused at my happiest memories – playing with my mum and dad, with Sorella, and, yes, seeing Ella. I felt a rush of power, and opened my eyes.

Recite the spell. Pas said.

What spell? I asked, focusing on controlling the energy while closing my eyes.

He didn't reply, but sent me certain memories of his. It showed him reading some spell that could give power to the reciter and one other person to destroy all darkness. *Could it really be that simple?* I thought.

No. Pas said. *It is very complex, more difficult than any other spell I have every tried. You may not be able to do it.*

Thanks for the vote of confidence. I sent for backup. *Arcus,* I called one of the Plant Elementals, *there's an Anima Tueur. I am going to perform a spell. Cover me.*

On it, came the reply.

I started the spell. Pas was right. The scroll that Pas showed me described not only the words of the spell, but also the actions that must me done while reciting it. It described the life of the Dark One (a.k.a., Malvagita), and the life of the Anima Tueur (in general, Anima Tueurs just suck on the souls of people). Then, it started harnessing the Energy that I had (which was a lot, to say the least), and making sure I could control it at all times. I recited the last line, and opened my eyes. I drew my second sword (I just had one sword in my hand), and yelled, "Páo!" The swords flew out of my hands, and stabbed the Anima Tueur in the heart and the head at the same time. "Éla." The swords flew back into my hands. I turned to Ella, and I did not like what I saw.

Ella was still trying to hold off Malvagita, who seemed like he had an endless supply of magic, and Cattiva, who looked ready to collapse. Ella also looked like she was going to collapse but she didn't back down.

"Thráfsi!" I yelled. I walked forward, and said, "Ella Elementa, sas díno aftí tín exousía. Déchesthe?" Translation, Ella Elementa, I give you this power. Do you accept?

"Apodéchomai tous, Stren Elementa!" She yelled. My hands glowed, and a beam of white light shot towards Ella. It hit her on the chest, and she gave a start. Then, straightened her spine, and glared at Malvagita. "Leave, Ubella. You have no business here."

Malvagita smiled. "You cannot tell me what to do, my dear." He waved his had, and all the Skión disappeared, reappearing behind him. The Elementals gathered behind us as well. "I have the all Leaders of the Elementals." The Leaders appeared. "I control them. You must obey me."

Ella smiled dryly. "Very ingenious, Ubella. However, I wish to correct one of your mistakes."

"Oh?" Malvagita said softly. "And what might that be?"

Ella raised her arms and summoned the Elements. "You have only twelve of the leaders. The thirteenth is not within your grasp."

Malvagita only smiled wider. "Look." He showed us the thirteen Leaders. What was Ella playing at?

"I see only twelve leaders and one Elemental. Yes," She said as Malvagita's expression went from confusion to comprehension to rage in one second. "I am an Elemental Leader. I am *the* Elemental Leader. And you, Malvagita Ubella, are going to leave this world once and for all."

Chapter 20

She attacked, and Malvagita parried. They engaged each other in a deadly dance. I felt the substitute leaders gather their strength. *Stren,* I heard Sorella tell me with her MindSpeech. *Help us.*

I understood what they needed. I supplied the energy, and the mist. Then, suddenly, they released the spell, and aimed a blast at the leaders. The spell released them, and they leapt away. I glanced at Malvagita and Ella, but they didn't seem to notice. I joined the fight, as did Cattiva. I just sent a blast of energy, which he somehow managed to deflect. Fortunately, I always think of backup plans. The bolt of energy took a more solid form. Actually, it took three solid forms. I left, leaving Cattiva to fight three beings that wouldn't die.

I turned back to Ella, and what I saw turned my vision red.

Ella was on the ground (With one of her swords in her hand), and was trying to stop his sword. He gave a lightning fast slash, and Ella gave a yell. She dropped her sword, and Malvagita leaned forward. "You never knew when to give up, Elena. You could have been successful."

"She says – she says success is not this monstrosity that you want, and that she already is successful."

Malvagita raised his sword to deal the final blow, and I yelled, "Ubella!" He turned, and I sent a powerful blast of energy at his chest, knocking him off. He dropped his sword, and I drew both of mine. I yelled, "Elementa!" A ball of Elemental Energy flew at Malvagita, but he only laughed. "Later, then, Elementals." He said, and vaporized. I turned, and saw that Cattiva had disappeared as well.

I ran to Ella's side. "Are you alright?"

She laughed weakly. "Yeah, nearly cut up to pieces, but alright. Joking," She said, catching the look on my face.

"Idiot." I said, thoroughly annoyed. "Sanare." I healed most of her wounds, and made her sleep. I tried to stand up, but stumbled. "Good to see you again," I said, looking at Juliet and the other leaders whom I had seen previously. Then, I blacked out.

Chapter 21

When I woke up, I had a throbbing pain in my head. I groaned and sat up. I heard someone else groan as well, and I turned. It was Ella.

"You O.K.?"

She glared at me. "Oh, definitely, Stren," she said sarcastically. "I feel like an elephant walked over me, but, oh, I'm absolutely fine."

She didn't get the power. Pas said.

What!?!

She didn't get the power.

How?

There's a special procedure for this acceptance of power.

Shall I do it now?

Yes.

I got of the bed and started dragging myself over to Ella's bed. She came over to me as well. We grasped each other's hands, and I started a spell. This spell was similar to the last one, except it described the First Battle of the Elementals. I talked about the near defeat that the Elementals had. I talked about how, when defeat seemed at our doorstep, When I was done, I said, "Ella Elementa, sas díno aftí tín exousía. Déchesthe?"

"Apodéchomai tous, Stren Elementa." There was a bright light, and a white force field materialized around us. The light died down, and I looked at Ella. I gasped.

All the cuts and bruises and various other wounds were healed. I glanced at my arms, and it seemed that the same was true for me. I got up, and pulled Ella up as well. "Let's go out, shall we?"

We went out, and I realized the force field had died down. We saw the Seven as soon as we got into the sun, and they ran up to us immediately.

Pianta shook her head. "One minute you're unconscious, and the next you're up and performing the most complex spells. What is wrong with you?"

"Nothing, really." Ella said, smiling mischievously. I saw Sorella walk up to us.

"Are you completely alright?"

"Absolutely." I replied.

"Good." She said, drew back her hand, and punched me. "Don't ever do that again, Stren Majier Elementa. Am I clear?"

"Crystal, 'La."

"Don't call me 'La!" Everybody started laughing.

"C'mon, Sorella. Let's see the Leaders. Where are they?" I directed the last part to the rest of the seven.

"Auditorium. You two better come back to the training area in five minutes."

"Who two?" Sorella asked.

"Stren and Ella. I think the Leaders want to train with you."

"Oh, okay." We went to the Auditorium. The Elementals were training, and I prepared myself for a long wait. Ella took the easy way out.

"Hey, guys!" Everybody turned towards us.

"And girls!" A girl yelled.

Ella rolled her eyes. "And girls. Good to see you all!"

Juliet ran towards us. "How are you?"

"Brilliant, how are you?" Ella responded.

"Same. Train a bit?"

"Nah, the Seven want us to train with them."

"Mmmh. Sorella?"

"I'll come."

I butted into the conversation. "Um, introductions?"

Juliet yelled, "Shut up, everybody!" Everybody stopped training. "Guys, this is Stren Elementa. Stren, these are Gabriel Tierra, Feira Le Feu, Mojada Auga, Luftal Lucht, Arbre Jeune, Fleur Bluma, Sol Soliel, Bogen Regen, Luna Mond, Steine Kostbare, Teire Animaux and Stella Estrella. Figure out who's who."

We had some small talk, and then Ella said, "Gotta go; the Seven want to train."

"See you."

Ella grabbed my hand, and we teleported to the training area. "Hey, guys." Ella said casually.

"What was that spell that Stren did that day?" Stervia asked.

"Gee, thanks for the warm welcome." I said.

"That's not an answer. What was that spell?"

Do not tell them.

Why not?

Swear it.

I scowled at him (Spiritually), and gave the oath.

"Well?" Stervia asked a third time.

I grinned cheekily. "That's for me to know and you to speculate about, because I have made certain oaths to prevent me from divulging that information."

Stervia muttered, "Idiot." I grinned even more.

"Something about training?"

They (The other five; Ella just rolled her eyes) nodded wordlessly.

"Well, then let's train!" I yelled.

We trained.

Chapter 22

Those two weeks, I actually learnt what 'normal' Camp life was like. Ella offered to relinquish the leadership of Camp, but Juliet said that the entire camp was looking forward to the traditional method.

"You don't want to disappoint the Campers, do you?" Juliet said with a cheeky smile. Ella just groaned.

"What's the traditional method?" I asked. They ignored me. I asked Pas, and he ignored me. Brilliant.

The first weekend, someone had stuck posters all over the place. This is what they were like.

The Traditional Duels!

Tomorrow, at sunrise,

The Elementals

Ella Elementa, Juliet Elementa, and Stren Elementa

Will duel for the Leadership of Camp Elemental.

Come one, come all, to the Auditorium in order to witness the duels.

I read the sign five times, and stormed to the Magos Verdaderos.

"What is the meaning of this!?" I yelled.

The girls had the nerve to look confused. "Of what?"

"This!" I said, pointing to the wall. Someone had managed to get in and put the posters there as well. They read it quite a few times themselves.

Ella turned to Juliet. "Well?"

Juliet shrugged. "You can't expect them not to make it a big issue. It's the first official duel in two years."

Ella frowned. "You were there for the last." She stated it as a fact. Juliet nodded wordlessly. "What happened?" Ella asked.

Juliet took a deep breath. "When I came to camp, there was another Elementa. He seemed nice at first, but later, we found some… disturbing things about him."

I asked, "What things?"

At the same time, Ella asked, "We?"

"Stella, Stein, and I found that he – well, he messed with the Dark side too much. They expected me to challenge him to a duel. I…I had no choice. He almost defeated me. Then, I remembered a spell I had read about the previous day, and cast it. It threw him out of camp, and then I took over. Stella, Stein and I revealed what we had found out about him."

"Do we know him?" Ella asked.

Juliet nodded. "Mauvaise."

Ella gasped. "Cattiva Mauvaise?" Juliet nodded. Ella looked furious. "He was a White magician, and he betrayed camp?" She snarled.

"Calm down, Ella. You saw his Amulet. As soon as I found out, I realized that he had disguised his amulet five days after I got to camp. He'd started then."

"Forget that." I said. "Who put my name for this stuff?"

"It is necessary for this position." Juliet replied.

"What do you mean?"

"All the Elementas must compete if there is a question of leadership."

"But there's no question. I want to relinquish my post to you, Juliet!" Ella said.

"It doesn't work that way. And if you two give up now, it will seem as though you are afraid." Ella and I groaned.

"I'm gonna go train. Coming?" I said.

"Yeah." Ella said. "Juliet?"

"No can do. I have to go with the leaders."

"See you." We left.

Chapter 23

The next day, I woke up when it was still dark. I donned my armor, put on my belt, charged my amulet, and went to the Auditorium. It was jam-packed. There was no empty seat. It seemed as though they took the 'Come one, come all' seriously. Ella was already there. We went to the Stage. Juliet came up a minute later. Soon, the first rays of sun hit, and the crowd cheered. Pianta and Cielo stepped forward.

"Thank you all for coming, Elementals!" Pianta said.

"Today, we will find out for sure who is the leader of Camp!" Said Cielo. The crowd cheered again. I caught a glimpse of a 'Stren Elementa', a 'Juliet Elementa', and an 'Ella Elementa' sign. My heart thudded louder as I scanned the audience.

"The first duel," Pianta announced, "is Juliet against Ella!"

More cheering.

I didn't actually pay attention to what was going on, but when the duel finally ended, I found that Ella had won. Juliet had a second chance against me, though. I got up, and drew my swords.

We (Juliet and I) circled each other for about ten seconds. Juliet shifted her position into an offence position, and I shifted into a defense position. She struck, and I yelled, "Stamatíste!" She stopped mid strike, and growled, "Versie." I felt some opposition to my spell, and I said,

"Stamatíste." The opposing spell stopped taking effect. "Páno." Her sword flew out of her hand. "Stamatíste." This time, it was to stop her flow of magic until something Dark attacks. "Ruhe. Do you accept defeat?" She raised an eyebrow. I sighed. "Just nod or shake your head, Juliet." She nodded. "Sie können sprechen." I said.

"So, Elementals," announced Pianta. "Juliet is now out of the contest! No offence," she added.

"None taken." Juliet replied.

"So," Cielo continued. "The result will be seen in this duel, between Ella Elementa and Stren Elementa."

"Now," said Pianta, "the last time these two dueled ('officially'), it was a draw. It will be interesting to see the final."

"The contestants will be give ten minutes preparation time. In the meantime, we will see the past unofficial duels."

I left before they did their commentating.

I saw Ella meditating, and started going towards her. I felt a ripple as I went through. Before I could react, Ella had leapt up and placed her sword at my neck. "Oh," she said, and lowered her sword. "It's you."

"Me." I agreed. We were silent for some time, and stared into the horizon. "Prepared?" I asked.

"Do I need to be?" Ella said, cracking a smile.

"Yeah. It won't be so easy this time."

"Oh, really? Want to bet?"

"Sure, if it's easy-"

"I'll give you more training. If I win-"

"No, if it's difficult."

"Are you saying there's no chance of you winning?"

"Odds are about one in a thousand. So, if it's difficult, what?"

"You get more time off."

"You're on." I said. We went to the Auditorium. Pianta was just finishing her speech.

"…So, it seems as though the odds are in Ella's favor, but who knows? Sometimes, Elementals win in the most bizarre ways!"

"I think," Ella said, "that I have prepared for some pretty bizarre situations myself, Pianta." the crowd laughed.

"Well," Cielo added, "we Elementals are looking forward to a brilliant duel! Get into position!" I moved to the north side, and Ella went to the south. "Begin!"

Ella struck at once. She ran forward, whispering some things under her breath. She then yelled, "Elementa!" Her swords blazed with power, and I raised mine. "Elementis!" A ball of the Elements flew at her. It hit her sword, and was absorbed. "Mazépste," she said. She sheathed one of her swords, and extended an arm. "Vlépo." I whispered. I saw something gather in her hand. It flew towards me, and I instinctively raised my sword. It hit my sword, and expanded. I struggled, but it started covering me even quicker. "Stamatíste!" I yelled, somewhat desperately. Ella said something else, and I felt my spell stop. Just then, her previous spell finished taking effect, and I couldn't move my arms. "Do you accept defeat?" I nodded. "Stamatíste." I could move again. Then, there was the formal announcement. We left.

Ella looked disappointed. "What's wrong?" I asked.

"I didn't want to be the leader," she said.

"You're great at it, Ella." We walked for some time, and Ella took a turn. "Where are you going?"

She grinned. "Something about extra training?" I groaned. "C'mon, Stren. You need to keep the promise."

"Fine." I went to the training area, and trained.

Chapter 24

We went to the Magos Verdaderos late that evening, and stayed up trying to formulate a plausible plan to end the War. We knew we had to meet Malvagita and Cattiva sooner or later, and wanted to be prepared for every eventuality. We went to sleep at about eleven-thirty that night. When I woke up at seven-thirty, Ella had already gone out to train. I went to join her.

"Hey, Ella." I said. Ella was going against Pianta, Cielo, Stervia, and Sorella at the same time, while Lau and Selena went against each other.

"Paraísthisi!" Ella yelled, and a bunch of eagles appeared, and distracted her opponents. "Eínai stereá!" It was a roundabout way of capturing one's opponent or opponents. It basically makes the air solid and reflects any spells made in it, but does not protect the person inside. The eagles disappeared, and I realized that it was just an illusion. Pianta and the rest tried to break the barrier down with force, but it just bounced them back. "Stamatíste!" Pianta yelled. The spell bounced back and hit her. Pianta stood there, frozen. Cielo tried to summon mist, but it covered her too. Sorella tilted her head, and frowned. She held out her hand (she had gotten five other Elements already, and could also summon mist) and summoned six Elements and Mist. "Conteram!" She yelled, and Ella's eyes widened. "Stamatíste!" She yelled, just as the ball of Elements were about to hit Sorella. "Stamatíste." The spell died down, as did the enchantments holding Pianta and Cielo. "Sorella, wait. The rest of you, leave. Now." They fled. Ella saw me, and told me, "You too, Stren. Go train with the other five." I walked away, just as I heard vaguely heard Ella say something to Sorella.

When I caught up to the other five, they were in the Auditorium. "What happened?" Pianta asked.

"The barrier that Ella put up would reflect any spells cast by anyone inside it back at the caster. Sorella said 'Shatter' to break down the barrier, and it went back towards her. The result would have been… messy, to say the least." I felt sick by the time I finished the explanation. We were silent for a second. I broke the silence. "Ella said that I was to train with you guys for some time. Shall we begin?"

"Sure. The same way as Ella was doing?"

I shook my head. "I don't think I'm at that level yet."

"Too right you're not." A voice said behind me. I whirled around.

"Ella." I acknowledged. "Where's Sorella?"

"I told her to train with the leaders for some time. Come around, all of you. I found a spell recently. Lower your MindBarriers."

The others started, but I stopped them. "Why?"

"It's a very important spell. We can't just say it out loud for everyone to hear."

Pianta tilted her head. "Where's your Stone?"

Ella scowled irritably. "What stone?"

Cielo's hand moved towards her sword. "What does the spell do?"

"I can't tell you now!"

I reached out for Ella with my Communication Stone. *Ella, where are you?*

The reply came a moment later. *I'm in the training area. Why?*

Come to the Auditorium quickly. Don't ask questions. I severed the connection. I gripped the pommel of my sword casually. "I've cast anti-spying spells. We can speak freely." That was code for 'imposter alert'. Fake Ella didn't realize what was going on. I told the other five, *Ella's coming. This is an imposter.* Then, I said out loud, "Well, Ella? Aren't you going to tell us this spell you've found?" There was a loud crash. Selena and Lau turned. I reached out to Ella via the communication stone. *Well?*

I'm right behind you, dolt.

Is Sorella alright?

She's fine. Who's that? I saw fake Ella in my mind's eye.

We're trying to figure that out. Come up front. I severed the connection.

I saw Ella, and drew my swords. Ella did the same. The fake Ella tried to run, but the real Ella yelled, "Eínai stereá!" Fake Ella was captured. Apparently, she didn't realize it, and ran into the barrier. The moment she hit it, she transformed. It was a Skiá (Singular of Skión). Ella got rid of it quickly, and told us via her Communication stone, '*The Skiá got something right. I've got a spell. It helps in detecting anybody or anything within a meter of you. These are the words.*' She gave us a long spell, and instructed us on how to cast it. When we were done, there was a faint glow, which disappeared in a second. I wondered if I imagined it. I turned to Ella. "Now what?"

She grinned. "Now you train."

Chapter 25

It turned out that Ella had a different type of training in mind. She taught us to modify the Spells we had Cast (the 'detectors'), and checked our reflexes. I kept reacting slower than the others. As a result, I had to do some extra training. In the end, Ella just made me increase the diameter of the spell, which we had reduced to one-and-three-quarters sword lengths. She told me to keep it at two. I tried that, and it worked perfectly. She perfected the other's as well. Then we went back to normal training. When we were done, Pianta and Cielo walked up to us.

"Can we tell the other Elementals about the Spell?" Pianta enquired.

"No. It takes too much energy."

Cielo started. "But it hardly dented my resource."

"We've gotten even more powerful. It is dangerous for the average magician."

"What about those above average?"

"They haven't been doing magic for long enough." The other two nodded and left. Ella turned to me. "We need to set a schedule to train the other Elementals."

"Okay..."

"Let's go, dude!" She said, and dragged me out. We got to the Magos Verdaderos, where I drew a board where we could write the schedule. We finally finished the planning (It took more time than usual because we took a food break) and took it to the Auditorium. I called the Elementals, and we waited.

When they finally came, I zoned out until Ella finished explaining the plan. Someone asked, "Why does it need to be so vigorous?"

"There's a war going on." Ella said mildly.

"The war's over!" Someone yelled.

"The war won't be over," Ella countered, "until both Ubella and Mauvaise are dead."

There was complete silence. Then –

"Okay, people, go train. We'll leave the schedules here."

They left, and I went to Ella. "What happens when we're prepared?"

Ella gave me one of those smiles that made me glad that we weren't enemies. "We attack Malvagita Ubella and Cattiva Mauvaise."

Chapter 26

The next few days, we trained as hard as we could. It passed on uneventfully (Unless you include Ella teaching new spells to the Elementals, and those spells producing a deafening blast as eventful), and we soon got settled into the schedule. Most of my schedule was, surprisingly, teaching the other Elementals Prima Lingua. When I asked Ella about this, she said, "Two reasons: one, that you are one of the few who know the language; two, that it would be embarrassing for you to *not* teach when the rest of the Seven are teaching. Of course, there is almost as much time set for training." So, I taught, and trained, and taught, and trained some more, taking a few breaks in between to eat.

About two weeks later, Ella called the Seven to the makeshift planning area. When we reached, Ella was looking at the planning board, muttering to herself and shifting the pieces. "No, that won't work... That should do it... No, Then these will be lost...If Phoenix goes there... Then Nereid can go there... Aura gets here..." Well, you get the idea.

I cleared my throat. Ella said, "Come around, all of you." We went round. Ella took a deep breath. "We are as prepared as we will ever be. We need to attack as soon as we can finish this plan." She indicated at the board below. I glanced at it, and saw the pins had changed. Ella saw my glance, and said, "Phoenix is the Fire group, Nereid is the Water group, Aura is the wind group, Gargoyle is the earth group, Dryad is the plant group, Narthêx is the flower group, Iris is the Rainbow group, Plutus is gems group, Diana is animal group, Asteria is the stars group, Helius is the sun group, Selene is the moon group, and Septum is us." By 'us', she meant the Seven. I tried to register it, and we spent the evening planning. We finally finished formulating a plan late in the night (more like early in the morning, actually).

"When do we attack?"

Ella looked out at camp. "Tomorrow, in the day time. About, say, eight thirty. It's the full moon as well, so we have a slight advantage even if the fight goes on after sunset. Let's get some sleep."

"Wait, Ella. Where are they?"

Ella smiled wryly. "Where it all began. Where we got our powers. Aede Potentia."

There was a stunned silence. Then, all six of us started yelling, "What!" Ella cut us off before we could finish saying 'wh'. "Ruhe." She said. We glared at her. She sighed. "Don't want to interrupt their sleep," she said, gazing at the rest of camp. "After all," she continued, 'who knows when we will get back?"

And on that happy note, we went to sleep.

I woke up early the next morning, and saw that Ella was still asleep. I decided to let her sleep. After all, we had a big day (or days) ahead. I went to the training area, and saw the Seven (minus Ella and me) training. I decided to go join them.

"Hey, guys." The whirled round with their swords at the ready. They saw me and relaxed. "Hey Stren. Where's Ella?" Pianta said.

"Sleeping, last I checked."

Cielo snorted. "Up all night fussing over the smallest detail of the plan, more likely." I cracked a small smile.

"I'll go check on her," Selena said. "She needs to be up now anyway." I glanced at my watch, and saw that it was seven forty-five. My pulse quickened. *Only forty-five more minutes till the attack,* I thought. I glanced at the rest of the Seven, and they appeared tensed as well. Selena ran off. The rest of us continued training. Ella and Stervia came up to us fifteen minutes later, and sent them to wake the other Elementals. Ella and I trained some more. This time, it was a draw (thank God, I guess). It helped my confidence. Some time later, the Elementals arrived, fully clad in armor, weapons at the ready, and expressions hard. Ella went up and gave a short speech, and everybody cheered. She didn't ask me to do one, thank goodness. We set out at exactly eight thirty. We marched out about twenty meters north Camp, and Ella yelled, "Muur van Macht!" There was a slight glow, and a colorful wall of magic appeared. I remembered that it was the same way I'd gotten here. Ella took a deep breath and said, "Aede Potentia." The wall became pure white, and we marched forward into it.

Chapter 27

The first thought that came into my mind when we got through the wall was, *Dark.* Something about that place was not right. *Well, duh,* I thought. *The two Darkest Elementals are here. Of course it's Dark.* Ella yelled, "Tela!" The Seven brought their spears out. I guessed they realized that something was wrong.

The room darkened a second later. Of course, that's Malvagita and Cattiva.

Malvagita extended his arms to either side. "Welcome, Elementals. Now, how do like this place?"

Ella took on his conversational tone. "It's brilliant, except for one thing."

"Oh, and what's that?"

Ella leveled her spear at him. "It's too Dark."

"Well, what did you expect?"

"Nothing less, Ubella." I recognized the cue, and stepped forward, as did the rest of the Seven. Malvagita just smiled, and extended his hand. A spear just like mine appeared in his hand, except his was Dark. The tip was a black gem that I didn't recognize. The shaft was Lámpsi ánthi (impure, of course). I glanced at Cattiva, and saw that he had a spear identical to his master's.

"Now, do you really want to go through this unpleasantness? It would be much easier for you to just surrender."

"Not likely, Ubella." Ella said aloud, and said mentally, *Plan B.*

I glared at her mentally. *But-*

No buts, Stren. Look at his hands. I looked, and saw a small ring with a small black ball studded in it. I recognized it. It was the same ball that he stored the Energy from the Leaders in. *No, Plan C,* I said.

Stren-

There are two of them. There best be two of us.

Ella gave in, and told the rest of the Seven to alert the rest of the Elementals. Ella continued the conversation with Malvagita.

"I challenge you, Malvagita Ubella, to a duel. You have worked against the Light. Therefore, as the leader of the Dark, it is only fitting that I, the Leader of Light and host of Der Estre Magier, deal out the punishment."

I directed about the same speech to Cattiva. They both smiled.

"We accept." They said together. "Let it be a double duel." Malvagita continued. "If one of the duels get over sooner than the other, the winner may not interfere with the other duel. Let us swear our oaths. It shall be a duel to the death."

Ella and I swore together in Prima Lingua, after which Malvagita and Cattiva did the same. We went up to the dueling area (yeah, the place had a dueling area. I was surprised too.). The Elementals gathered round the area, so it seemed more like an arena. I turned to face Cattiva. We gripped our spears and made sure that it would be easy to get our swords. Ella pushed them up her sleeves, which seemed like a bad idea, but they disappeared. She told me the spell mentally, and I did the spell myself. Then, I got into position. Malvagita, however, yelled, "Wait!"

"What is it, Ubella?" Ella asked.

He gestured to the side, where there were two chairs. Ella's eyes narrowed. *Judges,* she told me mentally. "We choose Mikrós. Who is your chosen judge?" Mikrós was a twelve-year-old rainbow Elemental who sneaked in with the other Elementals. I guessed Ella realized it just now, and chose him to keep him out of trouble if things turned nasty. Before Mikrós sat, he did the purifying spell, and the chair went straight from Black to White.

"Chose one more of your own, for as you see, we have none else from the Living but ourselves." Malvagita said. Ella nodded and chose Antheia. I guessed that she wanted Antheia to protect Mikrós if something went wrong.

I got back into position, and saw the other duelers do the same. Antheia yelled, "Begin!"

The duel had begun.

Chapter 28

Ella and I helped each other subtly, which is to say she helped me. I couldn't have done what I did if it hadn't been for Ella. Oh, what did I do? Well, let's start at the beginning.

It started out pretty good, and started I used my spear much more than my Magic.

First mistake.

I started gaining confidence. That's when he changed tactics.

He locked my spear with his, and I twisted mine. His spear clattered out of his hand. Instead of getting horrified, he grinned evilly. "Péthane."

Die. Very subtle.

"Ti zoí!" Ella yelled, and a bolt of white light intercepted Cattiva's spell. They (the spells) collided with a huge blast, but I stood firm. The dust cleared, but Cattiva was nowhere to be seen. I sensed someone behind me, and whirled round. It was Ella. We turned and stood back to back. All was quiet for a while. Then, all of a sudden, Malvagita appeared out of nowhere and struck at me. I parried, and he disappeared. I froze, and raised my spear. I felt Ella do the same. All was quiet for a while. Suddenly, I sensed someone approach. I raised my spear in the direction I sensed that person, but there was no one there. *Invisibility spell,* I thought grimly. Ella contacted me.

This spell will modify the sensor spell. You can tell the exact position of anyone hostile. I'll teach you how to remove this when we finish this. I liked how she said 'when' and not 'if'. Anyway, she told me the spell. I repeated the spell, and heard Ella say the same thing. I could still sense Ella, but I sensed two other hostile people. There was one on my left, and one on my right. The one on my right was more powerful (don't ask me how I knew that; I just did.). So, I started turning towards it. Ella, however, stopped me. *Wait. If that's Malvagita, it would be better if I went there. After all, it's still my duel. And, well, you aren't powerful enough. No offence.*

I'll get offended later. I told her, and turned towards my left. I could see a humanoid shape right in front of me. I guessed that it was Cattiva, since it was holding two swords instead of a spear. Cattiva attacked, and I blocked it with no problem. He seemed startled, since he took a step back. I took advantage of that, and sent a blast of White magic at him. It hit him in the chest, and he fell down (Within my sensor spell's range, thankfully). I threw my spear with deadly accuracy, and it hit him square on the chest. Immediately, I felt like throwing up. *He's dead. Dead.* I stood there in shock. The White Elementals (Except Ella) drew their weapons and knelt. Pianta announced, "Hail, Stren Elementa, Destroyer of the Dark." I took my spear, and stepped out of the area. Then, I went to a corner, and said, "Rise." The rest of them got up and went back to watching Ella and Malvagita fight. I cleaned my spear and curled up in a ball. *He's dead.* I thought. *He's dead, and I killed him.* I stared at my hands in shock. As I sat there curled up, Sorella came up to me. "Hey, bro."

"Hey, 'La." She didn't say anything about me calling her 'La. She just scooted closer and put her arm around me. "You're cold!" She said in surprise.

I cracked a small smile. "What did you expect?" I asked weakly. Sorella looked at me a moment, and then held out her other hand.

"Warm up." She summoned some fire, and I brought my hands towards it. A few minutes later, I was warm and comfy. "Thanks." I told Sorella, and stood up. "Let's go and see what they're up to." I gestured towards the arena.

Sorella pulled me up. "C'mon, then." We walked back to the arena in silence. I modified my sensor spell (I made the range larger), and saw Malvagita. They both still had their spears, and were trying to hit each other. Ella was dripping with sweat, but she refused to give up. Malvagita seemed fine. Ella tried every single spell she'd read about, and a lot of the spells Estre taught her, but to no avail. Then, her eyes glinted. "Katharíste!" She yelled, and there was a blinding flash of light. When it died down, Malvagita yelled in frustration, then in pain. He threw down his spear, then his swords, then his shield, then – well, you get the idea. I looked at his arms, and saw that they were burnt. "Stama-" He started, but Ella yelled, "Ruhe!" He stopped speaking, and Ella raised her spear. "Conteram." His barriers broke, and she threw her spear. It hit home, and Ella collapsed. She was like that for a count of ten, and then she got up shakily. The rest of us Elementals knelt, and acknowledged her as a Destroyer of Dark. Then, we got up at her command. Estre came out of her.

"Katharíste." She said, and the entire place became pure. "Ella Elementa," she called. Everybody became quiet. Ella stepped forward, and knelt in front of Estre. "You have done a great service to the Elementals and to the Light today. Therefore, I think it fit to give you a Name and title befitting a Destroyer of the Dark. Does anyone disagree?" There was more silence. "Give me your sword, Elementa." Ella drew her sword and gave it to Estre. "Rise again as Lady Bianca Luminis, Destroyer of the Dark, Protector of the White." Ella got up, and Estre said, "All hail Bianca Luminis!" Ella – or rather, Bianca – turned and swore to serve the Light for the rest of her days. Then, it was my turn. Estre made the same short speech and named me Albus Patronus, which basically meant protector of White. That's what Ella's - Bianca's (Ugh, this is confusing) - name meant as well.

I finished swearing my oath, and we went to the head of the group of Elementals. I summoned the wall. "Muur van Macht! Casa!" We stepped into the Wall of magic, and went to camp. After that, we went back to normal camp life, and had loads of fun.

So that's the story. So now you probably know why there was news of some disturbances in various parts of the world. We still have some things to do, like retrieving some lenses that Ella told me about. They were in the place Pas guarded as Custos Cartis. But that's a job for later. Right now, if you think you're an Elemental, well, Camp's right here waiting for you!

About the Author

Sharada M Subrahmanyam lives among her books. Inspired by the books that she has read by her favourite authors, like Tamora Pierce, Rick Riordan, Christopher Paolini, and Allison Croggon, she wanted to create a world of her own. Her first novel, The Elementals: The Beginning and the End, is an ambitious foray into the world of novel writing. With her second book, she hopes to continue her journey.

She lives in Chennai with her parents. She argues that societies that has a place for stories will be occupied so much that there will be no place for terror. She loves to read and listen to music. Logic fascinates her and she is interested in the workings of the human mind.

She has off late developed a fasination for patterns and opinion formation on the net. She wants to study and work to take advantage of technology to create opinion to change the world.